Mountain Hideaway

Pete Thorsen

Released on Kindle & in Print

October 2017

All rights reserved. No part of this book may be reproduced or transmitted in any form or by any means, electronic or mechanical, including photocopying, recording, or by any information storage or retrieval system, without permission in writing from the publisher/author, except that brief selections may be quoted or copied for non-profit use without permission, provided that full credit is given. This book is a work of fiction. Names, characters, places, and events are used fictionally. Any resemblance to actual persons, living or dead is entirely accidental.

Chapter 1

"Man, we sure got battered by those two hurricanes, one right after another, didn't we?"

"We sure did. Glad I live well away from any coastline."

"Yeah, pretty hard to really prepare for something like that hittin' yuh. But we all have to worry about North Korea no matter where in the States that you live."

"North Korea certainly is a threat. I'm not sure just how much of a threat though."

"What do you mean? We know they have big nukes and we know they have missiles that could reach us. I would certainly say they are the most serious threat we face."

"Their leader is certainly full of bluster, and you are correct that they likely do have the capacity now to really hurt the United States. I just don't know if he would take that step. If he did, we would wipe out his whole country with South Korea's and Japan's help. He may hate us, but I don't think enough for him to commit suicide."

"Maybe you're right; we would certainly wipe him out if he did strike us. He seems crazy though, and crazy people can do crazy things."

"That is true."

"Oh, my wife is calling me for supper. I'll talk to you later Jack."

"Sure thing Ron thanks for calling."

Ron is a nice enough guy, but sometimes I tire of listening to him talk about this disaster or that catastrophe that is going to happen in the next ten minutes and destroy us all. Sure something could happen in theory, but the odds are always very small. Ron talks about being prepared but as far as I know, other than him buying a couple of guns, he has done very little to prepare. Which is his own business and of no concern of mine.

We used to be neighbors before I moved. Now we are a long ways apart, though we do talk on the phone on occasion when he calls me. I have thought about preparing for bad times, but I have approached it very cautiously for a couple of reasons. I only have so much money, and I have always been careful spending what money I do have and weighing each purchase with needs so spending money on preparations for something that most likely will never happen is not up on my list. I guess that is my big reason for not preparing for the apocalypse because it likely won't happen.

I have guns because I have always been a hunter and when younger like many kids, I was fascinated with guns. When I was old enough, I bought one, and that led to buying another and so on until I thought I had enough. And I do have a little food tucked away, enough to cover me if there is a blizzard or something. But I have a fair sized mortgage payment every month, and I have to watch my money carefully all the time.

I always have been careful with money, and that is why I had enough saved up for the down payment on this place. I have been working for the same construction company for many years. I did not like where I was living in a small apartment in the big city and when I had saved enough money I started looking for a house I could both afford and in a location where I would like to live.

When I found this place, which was a fixer-upper, I checked to see if I could transfer my job to this area. The company I work for is not nation-wide but does cover a few states. And it did work out. My offer for this house was accepted, and my boss helped grease the skids for me to transfer to this general area and keep my job with this company in my new area. I have much farther to drive to work now because my new house is out in the boonies but at least I have a good job, and now I can put my money into home ownership instead of rent payments.

The distance I have to drive to work is really worth it to me to be out on my own. Even after three years, I am still working on my house and the place in general. I have just shy of fifteen acres of land with my own well. When built this house was more of a cabin for part-time habitation I think, rather than for year-round living.

It had a metal roof with a cathedral ceiling in the great room. It had a big stone chimney but a regular wood stove instead of a fireplace. The stove was a better choice in my mind. Seven hundred and eighty-four square feet of living space plus a sleeping loft is small but suitable for a single guy.

It needed a whole lot of work when I bought it. Politely it would have been called rustic, but in real life, it was just crude inside. But it was livable enough while I was working on it and I am still working on it to a lesser degree. I feel it is way better now and I know I could sell it and make some good money on the place. And I do think about selling sometimes.

I could sell and use the profit for a big down payment on a bigger, better place. Maybe another fixer-upper with more land and a bigger house. But I can make the house payments here without trouble, and I bought the place originally because I liked the house and the location. And now with all the hard work I have done, it looks good and I finished it off just the way I wanted to for me, not someone else.

The loft was about useless when I bought it. It only had a home-made vertical ladder going up to it. Now it has a nice stairway with a railing, and the railing runs along the loft edge so you don't feel like you will fall off when you are up there. The loft is now my bedroom, and it works out well for me.

The kitchen was almost non-existent when I moved in, and that is where a lot of my time and money has gone into. While still rather compact, it is now a nice kitchen with everything a person needs. No dishwasher though but with just me here that is fine. If I did decide to sell, I would remove one cupboard and install a dishwasher in its place. I set it up for a dishwasher when I re-did the kitchen area but never installed one just for myself.

When I bought the house, the only heat source was the wood stove. Which did and still does work well for heating the place. But now I have two small non-electric propane wall heaters that are fully capable of heating the whole house if I am away or for any reason, I don't want to use the wood stove.

I have a good supply of firewood. I cut my own on the national forest land every year. I get a permit, and while the wood is not the best for heating because it is almost all pine, it is also almost free except for the labor and fuel and the small permit fee. I also burn scraps from anyplace I can get them. Jobsites yield many dimensional wood lumber scraps that work very well in the wood stove and that is what I commonly burn.

I also knock down and burn wood pallets. Some of those come from job sites and some come from local businesses that give them away. The pallets have hard wood which lasts longer when you burn it compared to soft wood like pine.

After I had gotten some of the work done on the house, so it was more livable, I started actively seeking part-time weekend work to bring in more money. Mostly handyman type jobs and now through word-of-mouth, I have all of that kind of work I want to do. Word got around that I did good work at a fair price. I could maybe get enough of that work to stop working at my real job, but I do not think I will take that step. At least not yet.

Instead, now I am a little choosier about these side-jobs I do take. I have met many other handyman types that do the same kind of work, and I recommend one of those guys when I turn down a job. And sometimes one of them will throw a job my way. It seems to work out well enough for all of us.

The area where I live has many pluses I think. No big urban area nearby. It has lots of big game in the form of elk and deer. Nice scenery with lots of public lands, most of which is National Forest land. Not much in the way of small game though there are some rabbits around and some turkeys too.

I do like it here. And I am really happy that I bought here when I did because property values have really gone up just in the last couple years. I doubt that I could ever buy here now if I did not have this house already. That is one of the things that is stopping me from selling this house for a big profit. If I sold, I would have to move to a different location entirely. Or go back to apartment living again. Which is not a bad thing. Just not something I am ready to do right now.

So I will just be content with my little house here in the foothills. I have National forest land on two sides of my property so no one will be building any houses on two sides of me anyway. I hunt deer each year by just walking right from the house. I have the land cleared completely close around the house, so the threat of a wildfire taking my house is much less. A fire might smoke me out, but a wildfire is not as likely to burn me out.

Yes, my place has many things I like. Actually I cannot think of anything I don't like about my place here. The house could be bigger, but I live here alone, so it does not have to be bigger. A bigger house would really only be for show. My small house is very functional and much easier to heat than a larger one would be. I am happy here, and the only reason to sell it would be to cash out on all the equity I have built up here by fixing it up. And that just is not a good enough reason to move.

Chapter 2

Now with most of the work done to this house I have saved up some money, so I have a fair-sized 'emergency' fund. Just in case something comes up or I lose my job, or whatever would constitute an emergency for me. I have also paid ahead on my mortgage. I am now sitting better financially than I ever have been in my life. It is a pretty good feeling.

I have also started thinking ahead for the first time in my life. Always in the past, it was hard to think past the next rent payment or the next mortgage payment. Now I can actually start thinking about my future and what it might hold for me. And what I might want in my future.

One future thing that I have been thinking about is a family. A real honest-to-goodness family. Like having a wife and maybe a couple of kids. It has been a long time since I have even been on a date so this is more like long-distance thinking well into the future. I dated some when I was in high school and shortly after school. Nothing serious though, just teenager dating.

Since then I have not really met anyone, and I have made no real effort to meet anyone to date, mostly because of lack of money. Dating costs money. And I just never was anyplace for the most part where I could meet a single woman my age. I'm not into the bar scene. Before I could not afford it and now the closest bar is many miles away, and I just am not interested in drinking and wasting that money.

I'm not against people drinking, and usually, I keep a few beers in my refrigerator. And a cold beer does taste good after a hot day at work. But for me, one beer is enough. I have never acquired a taste for hard drinks. Well, that is really not true. I just have hardly ever tried any hard drinks of any kind.

So I have just started thinking about women again, and I think I am a nice enough looking guy. So if I did happen to somehow meet a woman she might not run away because of the way I look. My job is all hard work, and so my body stays lean with plenty of muscles. I keep my hair cut pretty short just for convenience sake. I am six foot one inch tall with dark hair. I shave just about every day, but because my beard comes in dark it always seems to look like I haven't shaved in a couple of days.

I don't drive a sports car, and I guess a woman that would be attracted to a man just because of the car he drives is not the one I am looking for anyway. So maybe just because I am ready to find a soul-mate, my chances of finding her are pretty slim. Time will tell I guess.

My mind drifted back to my last phone call with my old neighbor Ron. The doomsday guy. I wondered again if there was anything to the whole doomsday scenario. I don't live in a vacuum, so I know the whole world has many problems. And I know that many more people seem to be grabbing onto the doomsday merry-go-round.

The two recent hurricanes to hit America are a dramatic point that bad things can certainly happen. But there will never be a hurricane around here. Maybe a tornado but even that is very unlikely. There is the ongoing problem with North Korea that has been happening for decades. Granted it seems to be getting much worse, but I just don't see it going anywhere. The United States could crush North Korea like an ant under our feet. Their leader obviously knows this to be a fact. So I foresee a lot of bluster on both sides, but that is about the extent of it as far as I can tell.

So what else is there to bring on doomsday? A war with Russia or China or even both at the same time? It is always possible I suppose, but I really think that is very unlikely to happen. It just makes no sense from any angle, and all parties involved know this so, no, world war three is just not likely to happen.

Sorry but I just can't get into the whole doomsday thing even though it seems somewhat popular now. We could get a blizzard bad enough here in the winter to keep me home for awhile, but that is why I do keep some extra food on hand. That and the fact I hate shopping so I do it as seldom as I can. I think I can safely put the doomsday scenario out of my mind and concentrate on real issues instead. Like whether I should have the oil changed in my truck or just do it myself.

The company I work for just got the bid for a big expansion of the local high school. It is a year-long project at least I think. The project is set to start in the spring. Not too far to drive and steady, relatively easy work. Maybe things are looking up for me. Maybe I'll even meet a pretty school teacher who finds me irresistible. I can dream I guess.

There is plenty of work with the company and it even continues over the winter months. Most of the work is relatively easy anyway, and the school job when it starts will likely be even easier. The work is easy enough, so I have plenty of energy to take some additional weekend jobs. One such job I recently took just because it is only about two miles from my house. A woman called me and wanted someone to assemble the green house she had purchased. A simple enough job and because it was so close to my house I bid it a little lower than I usually would have.

The woman is strikingly pretty too which helped induce me to lower my bid some. I got the job and completed it quickly, and she seemed happy enough with my work. But that was it. No batting her eyes at me or anything. She was strictly business. I never saw hide nor hair of any husband, and though she did have two vehicles, they were both home each time I went to her house. And I did notice there was no ring on her finger.

I thought no more about her though after the job was done. I had plenty of other jobs to keep me busy. It was about three weeks later that she called me about another job.

"Mister Peterson, this is Amy Blackstone. You put up a greenhouse for me about a month ago. I have another project that needs doing if you are interested."

"Sure I'm interested. Let me know when I can come over and I can give you a quote."

"I don't think a quote is required. I had checked up on you quite thoroughly before the last job, and many speak highly of you. I was also happy with the little job you completed for me. I trust you will give me fair value. Can you still only work on weekends?"

"Yes, I have a full-time regular job, Ma'am. I do live pretty close to your place, and if needed I could likely do some work in the evenings if that would help."

"I don't know if that would be necessary Mister Peterson, but I would like the job started as soon as possible."

"I could stop by tomorrow after work, and you can let me look at what you want to have done. Would tomorrow work for you?"

"Yes, that would be excellent."

"Fine, I'll see you tomorrow about five-thirty then."

"Thank you. I'll see you then."

Then there was click before I could say goodbye to her. After the call was over, I realized I had no idea just what the job would be. Oh well, I would find out tomorrow night I guess.

The day at work was the same as any other day working. I guess the only exception was the fact that I was thinking about my meeting that evening with Amy

Blackstone. It should have been just another simple handyman job for raising additional cash, but somehow it seemed more than that.

    Or a much more likely scenario was just that I was hoping that this job would be more than just another simple handyman job. Or that it would lead to something much bigger. She was quite pretty, so I could hardly blame myself for trying to build it up to be more than it really was, being just another job.

Chapter 3

"Good evening Ma'am. What can I do for you?"

"Hello, Mister Peterson. Let's talk outside, and I will show you what I am thinking about having done."

We both stepped out and stopped in front of the house.

"I like my house, but it is rather plain in front. What I was thinking about was adding some kind of architectural feature to the front that would be pleasing to the eye and also have some practical use."

"So what did you have in mind?"

"I would like simple boxes made that are around six inches thick that come up about four feet. Then fill these boxes with dry sand to have a sizable mass that would help keep the house a more even temperature inside. On the outside of these boxes, I would like to have some of that manufactured stone so at a glance it would appear the stones were filling that whole space."

"I could certainly see that it would dress up the house to have a rock face halfway up the front wall. I'm not sure that you would realize any benefit to having the six inches of sand though."

"I had thought about just having the space empty, but that seemed a waste so even if it does not add much real value I would like them filled with dry sand."

"Sure that is not a problem at all. And I have worked with that fake stone in the past and would have no trouble doing the job for you."

"Thank you, and I do appreciate you mentioning the fact that I might not get any practical value from the sand. When can you get started?"

"I have no job set up for this weekend, so I could start it Saturday. I will have to purchase the wood to make the boxes and likely have to order enough of the stone."

"Would you like some money up front to cover the material costs?"

"I don't think that is necessary, Ma'am. I think we both trust each other enough so payment can wait until the end of the project. I'll keep all the receipts to give you with the final bill for the materials and labor."

"That would be fine. But know if you need money at any time during the job I will certainly pay you for materials and for the labor already invested by you."

"Thank you. Have you already checked for colors and styles of the manufactured rock?"

"I did look at a couple of samples, and I just want the one they call 'mixed river rock.'

I had a tape measure on me, and I made some measurements, and we went over exactly where she wanted the work done and how high and we discussed how I would work it around the few windows and doors that would be impacted by the work. This took some time until we were both satisfied that we were in complete agreement about exactly how and where everything would be done. It would be a fair sized job and take maybe a few weekends to complete.

I enjoyed spending the hour or so talking with Amy. I was some impressed with her knowledge of what she wanted done and how to do it all. And like the other times, I had seen her, I found it difficult to look away from her because I was captivated by her beauty. If she found my staring to be irritating, she said nothing about it. But I suppose anyone who looked as nice as she did was used to men staring at her.

Friday after work I stopped and bought most of what materials I would need for making the wood boxes. Saturday I drove over to Amy's place and started the work.

Putting the boxes together was done very quickly. I had thought about having a load of sand delivered but decided it would be much cheaper if I hauled the sand myself in my trailer. I was able to get to town in time Saturday to get the sand loaded in my trailer.

Back at Amy's, I was able to fill two of the boxes on Saturday before I left for home. On Sunday I was back at it and filled the remaining boxes and installed the top lids on each of them. By the end of the day, all the boxes were in place, firmly attached to the house and filled with sand. I had put up building paper between the house siding and the boxes. The job was made easier by having the boxes four feet high. That way I could use full-sized four-by-eight foot plywood and not even cut the pieces. Of course, there was cutting and fitting around the doors and windows.

By the time I left on Sunday that part of the project was completed. I had ordered the fake rock, and I would pick that up and everything I would need to install it on Friday. So on Saturday morning I could begin putting up the rock face on the completed boxes.

The weather cooperated the following weekend, and I was able to complete the whole job in just the two weekends. Both Amy and I thought the completed job looked pretty good. The now hidden boxes added more depth to the rock face, and I think the added depth added greatly to the look. Not that I thought it really mattered though because Amy's house sat so far off the road that it could not be seen from the road. So to see the new rock face someone would have to drive up closer to the place. And I had never seen anyone else ever show up there in all the time I worked on the project.

"Thank you for a job well done. It looks even better than I hoped."

"You're welcome. I think it does look pretty good."

"I'm sure I will have other projects for you in the future."

"You know, we are almost neighbors, and I would be pleased to help you with projects as a neighbor instead of as a job. Payment would not be necessary."

"Thank you, and I do sincerely appreciate the offer, but I would prefer to keep it on a professional level."

"As you wish but know that it is a standing offer of help. And just so you know, I have helped several of the surrounding neighbors. We are well out in the country here, and I feel we should stick together and help each other whenever we are able to do so."

"I see your point, and I do agree with your argument in theory. But while I have the funding I would prefer to still pay for any help I receive."

"And I can fully understand that too."

We talked more, and Amy did not seem to resent my offer of free help. Naturally, as a man, I wanted to cultivate a relationship with such a beautiful woman. But I sure wouldn't push the issue at all. And I thought she was out of my league anyway.

Over the next couple months, Amy hired me to do several odd jobs at her place. I built and installed a rather remarkable amount of shelving for her. Some of the shelving she had drawn out so the shelves were a certain size and distance apart to fit certain items she must have owned. Other shelving she just had me build to more random sizes.

I also built a lean-to against the side of the big steel building she had on the place. The very large lean-to was filled with stacked firewood again with my help. She bought the firewood, and the sellers had delivered it with a dump trailer. She had it dumped near the lean-to, and I stacked it inside the structure. It was a large lean-to, and she bought firewood until the space was filled.

When the phone rang one day I was not surprised and instantly recognized Amy's voice.

"Mister Peterson (she would not call me Jack) this is Amy Blackstone. I have a question for you."

"Hi. What can I do for you?"

"Are you a hunter?"

"Yes. I hunt deer and sometimes other critters."

"Would you teach me to hunt?"

"I could do my best, but there would be conditions that you would have to meet."

"I'm sure I could accommodate any conditions you might impose."

"Maybe not. The first condition would be that you call me Jack. And the second condition is that I would not accept any payment."

"I must admit that you do drive a hard bargain. And if I were to meet those conditions you would teach me to hunt?"

"It would be my pleasure to do so."

"Very well. I will abide by those two conditions. Jack."

"Excellent. Do you own any firearms?"

"I do, but I might not have any suitable for this endeavor."

"Maybe I should stop by your place, and you can show me what you have, and we can talk about it and even start your lessons about hunting."

"That sounds like a very good idea. Instead of a cash payment would you at least accept a home cooked meal, say tomorrow night?"

"I would certainly enjoy a home-cooked meal. And tomorrow would be fine."

"Would six work for you?"

"Yes, six o'clock would be fine. I'll see you then."

"I'll see you tomorrow, Jack."

After I hung up the phone, I just stood motionless for an extended time. Then I actually jumped up and down and shouted my joy. Amy was breaking down the barrier she had put up between us. I had fully accepted that our relationship would never be more than just a professional and a client. Now she was openly changing that relationship.

No this was not a date, but it sure was a start. And I had noticed that she had worked alongside me on a few of the last projects. And I thought we had worked well together. There had even been a fair amount of friendly banter between us while we were working.

This just might work out to be something special. At least I had hope.

Chapter 4

I was like a teenager all day looking forward to the evening with Amy. I kept telling myself that I might have it wrong and I better keep cool when I went over to her house. Then the time finally arrived, and I drove over. And I surprised myself with how calm I was by the time I knocked on her door.

She answered the door and invited me in. She was dressed normally like she always was in jeans and a tee shirt. She still looked amazing to me though. We went into the kitchen and made small talk as she finished the meal preparations. The meal was every bit as good as the host was beautiful. We talked about everything except guns and hunting.

After the meal, we got down to business. She said she did have a rifle that might work for deer hunting and it surprised me when I saw it. It was an AR-10 style rifle in three-oh-eight caliber. It was scoped with an obviously expensive scope.

"You could certainly use this rifle for deer or elk hunting. It is plenty good enough. You would have to use a five round magazine in it for hunting though. Um, have you shot it before?"

"Yes, I have shot it many times, and it is quite an accurate rifle. I forgot about having to use a small magazine for hunting. I'll pick up a couple in the next week or so, that's not a problem."

"Well, that settles what gun you will use. It is not the typical hunting rifle encountered around here though. Some purists might be put off if they see you carrying that rifle, but we can just hunt around here so that won't be an issue."

We continued to talk about hunting. I went over many things including clothing and footwear needed for hunting. She had never hunted anything before. Amy said she did have plenty of clothing and boots suitable for hunting. She had no blaze orange gear which was required here for big game hunting. Again she said she would just pick up what was needed in town on her next trip.

Amy surprised me when she said she wanted to cut-up her own deer. I knew she could easily afford a hundred bucks or so the local butchers charged to process a deer. I asked her about it, and she said she just wanted to learn the whole experience. Fine with me. It would just be more time I could spend with her when we cut up and wrapped her venison. Better than a date because we would spend the whole time alone together.

We ended up spending the whole evening together just talking. It was pleasant for both of us I think. We also made plans to meet on the weekend and go out in the field for experience outside looking for deer sign and such. I was certainly looking forward to that.

Over the next couple weeks, we met a few times. Amy bought her over-the-counter deer license and the gear she needed for the hunt. We had made several hikes together and had seen deer each time. When the season opened, she was ready, and we hunted by just walking from her home.

The hunt itself was anti-climatic because we only hunted for less than two hours. We saw a few deer, and she picked the one she wanted. She only shot once, and the deer ran a few yards but then lay down. I had previously explained about giving the animal time to die, so we waited together for about a quarter hour while keeping an eye on the deer. It never moved, and we walked up to it. It was dead, and she had made an excellent shot. I congratulated her on her first kill.

The killing of the deer did not seem to bother her, but I noticed she did stroke the deer's neck for a couple of moments and she did seem somewhat melancholy after killing the animal. But she soon returned to her all-business attitude and demanded that she be the one to gut out the animal.

I had explained the process earlier and now offered advice as she did the job. There were no tears shed, and she accomplished the task with no problems. She did allow me to drag the deer back to her place for her.

I had expected a successful hunt, and I had some things ready and placed in Amy's large metal building. I made the cuts in the deer legs and inserted the gambrel and then hoisted the deer up off the floor using an old rope style fence stretcher that I had used many times for a deer hoist.

It was cold enough now in the fall so the deer could hang for awhile with no worry of spoiling the meat. Once the deer was up and hanging I was about to commence skinning the deer, but again Amy stopped me.

"Please I want to do every step so I both know how and have some experience doing it."

"That's fine. I just started to skin it myself out of habit. It's all yours."

Like with gutting the deer she started working with me advising on the way. She made many nicks in the meat until she got the hang of it and after a bit, the nicks were fewer and fewer. She was pretty good about not cutting holes in the hide as she did the skinning. She caught on quickly and soon there was a naked deer hanging in the building.

"Do we cut it up now?"

"We could, or we could let it hang overnight to finish cooling and do the butchering tomorrow. Some like the meat to hang for varying lengths of time. I have cut some up the same day and some after a couple of days. I prefer to have a very short hang time but like I said many feel different about it. The weather now is a very good temp if you want to let it hang for a bit."

"I don't know. What would you do if this was your deer?"

"I would likely take advantage of the weather being nice and wait and cut it up tomorrow. And I would likely let the instructor take me out for supper tonight."

She was quiet and just looked at me for a moment.

"I guess I should just do as you say because you know more than me about this. So if I were to let the instructor take me out for dinner tonight what time do you think would be best?"

She now had a very big and very pretty smile on her face.

"I think your instructor should maybe pick you up about six-thirty."

"I guess I better be ready at six-thirty then. Now the instructor should maybe go back home so I could make the transition from great white hunter to demure widow going out on her first date."

We were both sporting big smiles now, and before I screwed something up, I bid her goodbye and made my way home. Luckily there was no traffic on the back road to my house because I was not fit to be driving, even at the slow speed, I was driving. My head was on cloud nine, and I don't know if my feet even touched the ground after I got home because I was floating along with thoughts only of my upcoming date with Amy.

And now I knew that she was a widow, something I never knew before. She and I had talked many times, but she was always pretty careful, never mentioning much of anything about her past. Maybe this was because it would be painful to her or maybe she just wanted her past to remain in the past.

I was surprised when I had the nerve and asked her out, and then I was even more surprised when Amy had said yes to a first real date. Now I had to make reservations someplace and get cleaned up enough to not look like a country bumpkin out with a movie star.

Chapter 5

Evening finally came I went to pick Amy up for our dinner date. She was dressed to kill, and it did almost give me a heart attack. To say she was beautiful would be a gross understatement. We went to a way fancier restaurant than I usually ever would go to. I spent a ton of money, but I could have cared less. I was just basking in her presence. I have no doubt I was the envy of every man that saw us together.

I had never seen Amy dressed up before and she almost took my breath away every time I looked at her all night long. The evening was over way too soon, and I drove her back to her house. When I walked her to her door, she asked me in, and we went inside together. She asked if I wanted coffee and I accepted.

While the pot of coffee was brewing, she excused herself and when she returned she was dressed in well-worn jogging pants and a tee shirt. She still looked gorgeous to me no matter what she was wearing. We each had a cup of coffee. And we talked.

Amy finally told me some about her past. She was a widow and had only been married a very short time. When her husband had been killed in a small plane crash with a business partner, she had been devastated and had retreated from the world. Eventually, she had sold everything and bought this place well out in the country and in a different state.

She had made no friends here and kept to herself. She did not need to work because her husband had a large life insurance policy and it had a double indemnity provision which resulted in a very large payout.

We talked for a couple of hours. When I left, I kissed her for the first time when we said good bye. I would not be gone long because we had made plans to process her deer starting in the morning.

When I showed up in the morning things were good between us. It was almost like last night had never happened, and yet things were also different. We worked and cut up the deer. I did most of the cutting, and she did most of the wrapping, but naturally, she got involved in both to get the experience. It was work but I think we both enjoyed the time spent together.

Time passed, and winter came. Though Amy had enjoyed the dinner in the fancy restaurant, she would not allow me to spend my hard earned money recklessly on things like a meal out with her. So we would occasionally go to a movie together or have a meal in a café or often just hang out at her house and sometimes even at my house.

We were both afraid to move too fast, and we went slowly developing our new relationship. We were both very comfortable when we were together, and neither of us wanted to spoil something that could be so good for both of us.

By spring I thought we were both ready and I asked Amy to marry me. She hemmed and hawed around for awhile but it was just an act to tease me, and she finally said yes.

She did ask if it could be a simple small ceremony and I understood, and that was fine with me. The first week in June we were married. We talked about it, and I moved into her house. Mine was put up for sale and thanks to a short bidding war, was sold for a very good price. Together we changed the title to her property into both of our names. With what money she had and the profit from selling my house we were setting very well financially. I never considered quitting my job, and I had only taken a few days off for a very short honeymoon.

    I admit I was completely computer illiterate, but that was not the case with Amy. She was an internet warrior and spent a bunch of time on her laptop computer surfing the web. Amy also had a large garden and spent a fair amount of her summertime tending to her garden. She had turned her property into a fresh food grocery store when she had moved here.

    The big garden was only part of it. She had also planted or in some cases, had planted for her, a large variety of fruit trees. And she had not stopped there and had a large patch of blueberry bushes along with raspberry and blackberry bushes. She also had a couple of more uncommon plants like gooseberry and currant. Most of the fruit trees were still quite young, but Amy had spent the money to buy some that were quite a bit larger so she would have fruit sooner.

    Because of the elk and deer in the area, just after all the fruits were planted Amy had a seven-foot fence put up to surround all the fruit trees and berries. An underground water line was used to water the large orchard. I had never tried to grow a garden, but the fresh produce was certainly good to eat.

    Our life together was hard to describe and like nothing I had experienced before. I had to be careful coming home every day because I found myself speeding just to get home faster to see Amy. And it seemed I was not the only one that looked forward to me coming home every afternoon. Amy would often walk out and meet me as I was getting out of my pickup.

    I had kept my pickup, and we decided there was no need for having three vehicles, and we sold Amy's car. We kept her SUV because it was four-wheel drive and good for driving in the winter. She asked about me buying a new or at least a newer pickup but mine still ran fine and was very dependable, so I saw no reason to buy something different even though we could afford it.

We learned many things about each other. I learned that Amy had several guns and was an active shooter. She also had a carry permit and usually carried a concealed handgun where ever she went. I liked to shoot, and we often had impromptu shooting matches between us. The loser usually had to do the dishes.

I was now working at the school expansion job and stayed pretty busy. I had stopped doing any weekend jobs other than occasionally helping one of the neighbors. There were projects at home with Amy having many ideas on things she wanted to be done around the place. I also learned the real reason for the rock face she had put on the house. The sand filled boxes made the now protected part of the house virtually bulletproof.

Overall things could hardly be better for us. At least I thought so, but there were many things happening here in America and around the world and while I never try to keep track of what's happening everywhere, I do know that many things happening a long way away can have a direct impact on me. And such was the case this time.

The United States had been having trouble with North Korea for a long time. But in the last couple years or so that had heated up dramatically. North Korea had nuclear weapons for many years, but they had done a few tests recently with the last test pointing to a much more powerful thermo-nuclear detonation. At the same time, they had also tested several long-range and medium-range missiles. Most experts now agreed that North Korea now had missiles capable of reaching the US mainland. And most thought they had nukes that would fit on those missiles.

In response, through the United Nations, much more strict sanctions had been imposed on the rogue nation. But this seemed to be no deterrent to that nation. So the

United States, after receiving even more vile threats from North Korea had now placed even stronger sanctions against them. In the last non-UN approved sanctions basically stated that anyone doing business with North Korea would not be allowed to do business with the United States. This seemed to be directly pointed at China.

      Most thought it was just strong talk, but then several large loaded ships from China were not allowed to dock and unload in our ports. The ships were turned back and forced to return to China with the loads still on them. When this happened bad things started happening, and those things would have negative global impacts.

Chapter 6

No one in the world thought that we would ever stop doing business with China. After all, we depended on China to supply so many different things that were vital to our nation. But our President had made it plain that if China or anyone else did business with North Korea, they would then lose our business. China had called our bluff, and they found out that it was not a bluff at all. Instead, it was a fact.

Over the next three or four weeks there was a lot of talk between our nation and China. But neither side would back down. China was so sure that our President would back down......but then he didn't. Then came a flurry of threats from China that remarkably our usually out-spoken President did not even acknowledge. When finally China threatened all-out war our President responded with a simple statement. All he said was that he had his finger on the button and if China made any hostile military act he would push that button.

This time China took him at his word and did not think it was a bluff. There was no more hostile talk from China, but there was action. It came in the form of China dumping all their holdings of US treasuries. The value of the US dollar dropped like a rock. So China got paid for the Treasury notes with US dollars that were now worth a fraction of what they were just a week ago.

All of this did not happen in a vacuum. The whole world was watching and reacting to what was going on between the two superpowers. All the world markets were in turmoil. All stock markets were in freefall. Then all at once, it seemed no one wanted to accept US dollars anymore for payment. The US dollar the only world-wide currency turned toxic. Other countries that held US treasuries demanded payment. So they got payment in the listed amount of US dollars. The new way devalued dollars. What they ended up with was just pennies compared dollars.

World markets all collapsed. International trade ground almost to a halt. Everyone had always traded with US dollars, and now there was no good alternative. All the world's fiat currencies were looked at with skepticism. Not only did no one want US dollars but they did not want Yuan or Euros or any other currency. Some offered to trade in gold, but no one knew what value to put on the gold. It had always been traded in dollars too. With all currencies dropping in value and with no faith in any currencies all trade just stopped.

Ships like huge oil tankers with full loads did not know what to do and just stopped and floated on the oceans in the hopes this would soon be sorted out. It was the same for the large and small dry goods carriers. Some returned back to port, but many just waited off-shore of their original destinations.

With no international trade, the world just ground to a stop. The repercussions of no international trade devastated most countries. Riots erupted all across the globe. The great United States of America was not spared from this reaction either. It was a new world. A violent new world full of turmoil and strife.

And yes even the little Peterson homestead was effected.

I freely admit I had no idea what was coming. I had no idea that what was coming was even possible. If someone would have told me I would have called them a liar. Because I knew that it was impossible. I lived in the greatest nation ever. The most powerful and richest nation in the world. I was working full-time, and anyone who wanted a job could get one. Unemployment was at record lows. And I often saw help-wanted signs posted here and there.

I had the best life ever, with a beautiful wife who loved me and a good paying job that I actually liked going to every day. I had plenty of money in the bank, and our nice home was paid in full. We had two good vehicles and no payments of any kind. I did not know how my life could get any better. And I could not even see any shadows on the horizon.

When I heard that our President said that our nation would not do business with anyone who did business with North Korea I thought exactly what every other American thought. Yeah, whatever. Just another sanction, like all the others that had been going on for years. Ho hum just another day, move on to the sports scores.

It sure did not make a big slash on the news. It was just after a story of an abandoned trailer house fire and just before a feel-good story about a dog who found his owner after being lost for a year. In other words, it was just no big deal.

A couple of weeks or more later when we had all forgotten about it was when America refused to allow the Chinese ships to unload at our ports. That made the news, but again I was like other Americans and paid no attention to the short news story. I just wanted them to move on to the weather report which was certainly more important to me.

In the following weeks, there likely was reporting on the news about the arguments back and forth between the United States and China, but I honestly don't remember hearing those reports. I likely did but just paid no attention to them. In my defense, I have to say that it was partially Amy's fault. Even after being married for some time I can hardly take my eyes off her, and she usually has my full attention even if she is not talking to me and I am just watching her do the dishes or something. So you see I do have an excuse.

I'm not sure how long a time passed before China sold off all of the US Treasury notes they owned. I'm sure that made the news, but again if I heard it, I paid no attention. I think after that event things moved rather quickly. It was Amy that more or less then forced me to watch the news and even told me the scope of what was happening.

At first, I thought she was just joking, but I could see the fear in her eyes, something I had never seen before. That was what caused the big jolt to me. I then shut the news off and told her to explain everything to me. We went through a couple of cups of coffee while she explained what was happening and what was likely to follow. It was bad. Very bad. Like something, I could not believe.

Just Amy's visible fear gave credence to what she was saying. I knew for a fact that she knew more about how things worked in the world than I did. She had explained some things to me before. And I knew she spent a fair amount of time on the internet researching many different things. I also knew she had believed in the doomsday theory. She had told me before we got married and showed me what she had done to prepare. I was okay with that even though I did not believe in the whole doomsday thing.

Now after listening to her I was starting to change my mind. I was still having a lot of trouble wrapping my head around what she was saying. It just could hardly be true, but in my heart, I was starting to believe. Then she took me by the hand and led me to her storage area. It sure looked fuller than I remembered it. Then she said she had been ordering some more stuff.

After that, she led me back to the kitchen table and produced a notebook. We sat side-by-side so she could show me what she had written. It was mostly lists. A couple of lists of things to purchase, some of which had lines drawn through them that I rightly assumed had already been received.

A list of things that we could and should do to the place, mainly to make it more secure. I started reading the lists of things to purchase. It was long lists, and some of the items were, well, uncommon. And some were kind of scary, like the fifty caliber Barrett rifle. Which was also very expensive too I saw because she had estimated prices next to many of the items.

She had quit talking and just let me read. When I was done reading, she sat and waited for me to say something. I was overwhelmed by everything she wanted to buy so I just said the first thing that came to mind.

"I love you."

I guess it was the right thing because she just melted into my arms.

Chapter 7

"I think it is too late already to get much of the stuff I think we should have. I did buy quite a bunch of silver coins and some gold coins already. I don't know if they will ever be worth having, but the metal will always be better than the paper money."

"You think money will be worthless?"

"No one knows the answer to that. But it is pretty safe to say that it will drop down to have only a fraction of the value it has now. Are you OK with me trying to buy some of the stuff in the lists?"

"If you think it's for the best then I am with you all the way. What do you want me to do?"

"I'll make a short list of items that you can hopefully pick up locally. You can do that tomorrow if possible. Every day is precious now I think. Things will start to move much quicker. And as more and more people wake up the supply of everything will drop until there are shortages of almost everything."

"And you will be ordering things off the internet?"

"I will and in fact I will start that tonight. And I will make a trip to town in the morning and get some other things in town and stop a few places like the propane dealer."

"Is everything really going to all come to a stop?"

"I think so. Or at least sometimes I think so. Other times I think maybe it won't be so bad. But even then I think it is better to plan for the worst just in case that is what we get."

"I guess I agree. Better to be ready than just wish you were ready."

"I love you. But now I want to get to work."

She kissed me and then went straight to her computer. Soon she was absorbed in what she was doing and totally oblivious to me or anything else. I went over and watched for awhile. I didn't talk or touch her because I could see she was concentrating on what she was doing. And what she was doing was ordering stuff. Some of the amounts were what I thought was rather high, no like bizarre amounts of some things.

But I said nothing, and after a bit, I just left her to do what she thought was best for us. I went to bed and never woke up when she came in sometime during the night. But she was sleeping peacefully next to me when I got up in the morning. She was still asleep when I left for work. I did find the list she wrote out of the items she wanted me to buy today. I took it with me when I left for the day.

It was a regular day at work. After the talk, Amy and I had last night I expected everything to be different today. But it was the same as always. Guys talked about some sports team or about getting new tires for their truck. Just mundane things like always. And when I left work to do my assigned shopping everything was normal everywhere I went. I guess I expected something different. I was able to buy almost everything on the list so I figured Amy would be happy. And that was my biggest goal in life, just to make Amy happy.

When I got home, everything looked the same, and I carried in the stuff I had bought. Amy was on the computer but signed off when she heard me come in with my load of stuff. She came and gave me a kiss before she even said hello.

"Just set that stuff down and go get cleaned up. I thought I would take you out for supper tonight."

"If I go do I get another kiss?"

She just kissed me again and then swatted me on the butt to get me moving. After a quick shower and a change of clothes, she met me, and we went out the door.

"I'll drive because you worked all day."

So she drove to a hole-in-the-wall café that we went to sometimes. The place wasn't fancy but did have good food and was fairly close to our place, or at least closer than most places anyway because it was still fifteen miles each way. We had the typical good meal there and just made small talk the whole time. Neither of us talked about what was coming or anything bad. It was a nice relaxing meal, and I think that was Amy's plan. The waitress knew both our names and stayed to talk for a bit because the place was not busy at all.

Amy drove us home, and we did little talking and never listened to the news. Instead, we just cuddled on the couch before going to bed. In the morning I left for work, and it was yet another day just like any other. When I got home, I found two dump trailer loads of firewood had been dropped off during the day. I also noticed two new propane tanks now sitting alongside the one we did have. Once I walked over I could see that the tanks were indeed brand new ones and they were also filled and hooked up with our original one. Only then did I remember seeing them on one of the lists.

Amy had another thing she wanted me to buy if I could find them. She wanted at least two good metal drums suitable for us to store gasoline in for long time storage. I knew where I could buy those drums with no problem, but I would have to bring them home and then fill them using regular gas cans until both were full. Amy told me she had ordered something she called 'PRI-G' that should make the gas last a long time in storage. She said it was up to me to figure out a method to get the gasoline from the drums into whatever equipment we wanted to put it in.

And so it was for the next several days. I would go to work and find more stuff at the place when I got home that had been delivered during the day. I had brought home three drums, and I took all of our gas cans in every day that I worked and filled them on the way home to dump in the drums.

By the time a week had passed, I had noticed other people talking about what was happening. And driving past I noticed the grocery stores seemed to be doing good business every day. It was on a Wednesday that I came home and a couple of trucks were just leaving. I didn't notice anything and asked Amy what the trucks were doing here.

"They delivered the solar panels and started the installation. They will be back tomorrow and Friday too. They didn't know if they would finish on Friday or not. If not they will work Saturday. The guy said they were getting a lot of orders lately."

"So we will have solar power?"

"Yes, solar and a small wind turbine with a spare wind turbine in storage. The solar panels will all be on the roof of the garage, and I cleaned out an area in the garage big enough to hold the battery bank. But I think maybe you should build a separate lean-to or a small close building to house the battery bank when you get the time."

"How big does it need to be?"

"Come on; I'll show you."

So we went out to the garage and in an area in the back corner that previously had been a catch-all for junk we did not want to quite throw out was now cleaned out and several rows of new large batteries were in place there. There were a lot of batteries. And judging by the size of each battery I figured the installers most likely had used some kind of power equipment to move all of them into place there.

There were wires and a bunch of electrical panels on the wall but clearly not hooked up yet. It looked like a complicated set-up. One look and I thought the batteries would stay right where they were now.

"I'll just wall off this area of the garage, and we can leave the batteries where they are now."

"OK, I guess that would work."

Walking back to the house I saw yet another new propane tank lined up with the other ones. I did not bother to walk over there, but I just figured that it was full too. Amy pointed out the big pile of cardboard that had built up from all the deliveries that we had received during each day when I was gone to work. Amy must have been very busy every day just un-boxing and storing all the stuff she had ordered and got shipped to the house. I would have to load all the cardboard up and haul it to the transfer station on Saturday morning. I glanced again at the pile. I would have to use the trailer.

Chapter 8

"I have spent or moved most of our money."

"You mean what we had in the checking account?"

"No. I mean all of our money. I transferred all we had in the money market accounts into our checking account, and I closed our savings account. The checking account still has quite a lot of money in it, but that is because I left enough to make sure there was plenty for the automatic payment of the credit cards."

"Um, you didn't buy that much stuff did you?"

"Mostly the answer is yes. I converted the money into gold and silver which is now here. I also have about six thousand dollars in cash here at home too. And the solar and wind system is all paid for already. That was quite expensive, and I bought a bigger system than they recommended. The three new propane tanks and all that propane cost quite a bit too but that all went on the credit card.

I bought a lot of food but compared to everything else that did not amount to very much. We do have a big pile of silver coins now and a fair amount of gold coins too. And that big Barrett rifle came in with all the stuff I ordered with it. That is on the credit card also. I can't wait to shoot that big rifle as soon as we mount the scope on it."

"All of our money?"

"You're not mad at me are you?"

"No. I'm not mad at you, and I'm not sure if I ever could be mad at you. Mad about you is a totally different matter."

"You're really not mad?"

"No, I'm not mad at all. It was just a shock I guess because between us we had quite a bunch of money and when you said it was gone it was just a shock."

"There just wasn't time to close out our retirement accounts, so those are intact. Which is too bad because we will just be out all that money I think."

"You think so?"

"Yes. I'm pretty sure we will never see a penny out of those retirement accounts."

"That's many thousands of dollars!"

"Just count us lucky that we were able to save as much as we have. Because this happened so fast there is a paper trail of almost all the precious metals I bought. I hope that does not get taken away from us by the government."

"You think they would take it away?"

"They have before. Remember when they outlawed gold in private hands eighty or ninety years ago?"

"They did? Here in America?"

"Yes, they did. And they took it from citizens and gave them a set price for the gold they took. And the government set the price of course to anything they wanted. I believe it was thirty-five dollars an ounce if I remember correctly. They did it once and will likely do it again. I don't think they will take silver though. There is just too much to take from everyone. That is why I got mostly silver."

"This is really happening isn't it?"

"Yes, I'm afraid it is happening."

It was a shock that Amy had used almost all of our money, but I trusted her to do what she thought best for us. The solar company finished the solar setup and the included wind turbine. The wind turbine was on its own stand, not far from the garage. To keep the wire run short I imagine. It looks kind of neat spinning away whenever there is a breeze.

After we had checked out the new solar system for a week, Amy called and canceled our regular electric service. We did not have a grid-tied system. Amy said we had no time to get a system like that and we didn't need it grid-tied anyway.

I had a fair sized gas generator that I used on some of my weekend construction jobs in case we needed to add to our solar power sometime. With the solar system, Amy had ordered a very large battery charger we could use with my generator to charge the battery bank if we ever needed to but that was unlikely because we had wind and solar both.

And now we had four five-hundred gallon propane tanks all full of propane. And we had more firewood than we could use in at least two years, or more than likely three years. And that was if we used only wood and not the propane for heat.

And then there was all the other stuff Amy had ordered. Pails and pails of food along with almost countless gallon-sized cans of dried or dehydrated food. She had also bought three of the largest food dehydrators that she said she could find to use for our fruit and some vegetables. Most of the fruit trees were just now starting to produce. And in another year we would be able to harvest quite a lot of our own fruit from all the trees and bushes we had here.

Plus, we had her large garden. And she now had cases and cases of canning jars and countless boxes of lids, along with a new canner to go with the other one that she had been using. She had bought the biggest smoker that I ever saw other than home-made ones. She said that we would use that for all the meat from the deer and elk we shot.

And speaking of shooting, that huge Barrett rifle is incredible. I think we could shoot an elk a mile away with that thing. I never asked Amy how much the scope for that rifle cost, but it was likely a couple thousand dollars or more. It was pretty cool though. And we had cases of the fifty caliber ammunition. I bet that is at least five dollars every time you pull the trigger.

We already had plenty of other guns, but Amy had ordered in a huge amount of ammunition for each caliber we owned. She said she had thought of getting reloading equipment but instead just spent that money on ammunition instead. We did now have two matching AR-15 rifles with low powered scopes on them. She must have bought them in town I guess.

With the AR-15 rifles, once we sighted them in, we had a couple of competitions between us. Once we were both familiar with the rifles, I set pieces of firewood up at about seventy-five yards. Then with both us having a thirty round magazine in the rifle, we each shot as fast as we could accurately shoot to see who could knock the most pieces of firewood down the fastest with one magazine.

That was really fun, and I refuse to say who won the competition. Ammo for those two rifles was not a problem because Amy had got in several cases in that caliber. I don't know how many thousands of rounds we had for them.

I was still working every day and we were still on the school project though it was just about done. There was talk about maybe we would all be laid off when the project was completed. I don't know if it was just talk or not.

Things are really starting to happen now though. Many stores have bare shelves in them now. With no products coming in from China it seems to be affecting a lot more stuff than any of us thought it would.

Now that international trade is faltering many things like fresh food from South America is also missing from store shelves. That and the fact many people are buying up what food there is available is really making it hard on some people just to buy enough food to eat.

The prices on everything have skyrocketed an amazing amount. Even stuff from here and not imported. And gas is now over seven dollars a gallon. And it still goes up just about every day. Even lumber products are getting hard to find. Much of it comes from Canada, and I guess they don't want to take US dollars in payment anymore. At Amy's urging, I had bought up a pile of building products just to keep on hand while they were still available and at the old prices.

Today I see when I filled my gas tank that gas was now eight forty-nine a gallon. I wonder where it will top out where people just can't or won't pay any more for it.

Chapter 9

Unemployment is now way up. It went from around four percent up to eight percent in just one month. They speculate that next month it will be from twelve to fifteen percent. Amy thinks it will be in the twenty's by next month. And that number will include me. The school job is now done and we did all get laid off. I signed up for unemployment today. I did it on the internet. Well, actually Amy signed me up because I didn't have a clue as to how to do it.

There was no reason to drive to town and sign up, especially with gas now over ten dollars a gallon. Both UPS and FedEx had a joint announcement that they would be only delivering to rural areas now only once or twice per week because of fuel costs. Also, rates were now double with additional increases expected very soon. Amy says they will both close down within a month, two at the very most.

The list of business closings is not mentioned on the TV news. The local radio station listed all the closings they knew about today, and just the local closings amounted to a long list. Some of it was due to lack of supplies and merchandise because of no international trade. Some closings were due to the high cost of fuel. In some cases, the employees had to quit because with the high fuel cost it made no sense to drive very far to a job where you only made your gas money to drive to the job.

For Amy and me, we just stayed home. She had made a list of things she thought we could do around the place. She was good about making lists. For the first time closed the gate on our driveway. It was more of a symbolic gesture than a practical one.

I had looked at her list of things to do to make our place more secure. Obviously, some of the things she suggested would only be done as a last resort because they could have fatal results. I did make many of the mouse trap alarms she suggested. She had bought quite a bunch of the simple wooden base mouse traps for this purpose I guess.

Making the alarms was very easy. I only had to bend the bail (the part that traps and crushes the mouse) into a sharp vee shape. Then let the bail snap down on the wood base. This would put a big enough dent in the wood to mark where to drill a quarter inch hole in the wood. A quarter inch is about the perfect size to insert a standard shotgun shell primer. Amy had also bought three boxes of one hundred each of the shotshell primers from the local gunshop.

Once you put a primer in the freshly drilled hole, the trap is ready. A simple string can then be attached to the trigger on the mousetrap. If anyone touches the string, the mouse trap will snap shut and make the shotshell primer go off. The primer is surprisingly loud. I tried the first one to see if it would work. It did, but it also pointed out some problems with the design.

The trigger was way too light and had to be modified, so it was harder to make it go off. Also, the primer was both loud and powerful. The loud part was good, but the primer was powerful enough to split the wood base of the test trap, making it a one-time use. To counter this, I added another piece of thin wood (I used a piece of quarter inch plywood) to the bottom of the wood base. I glued it in place and also used a couple of screws.

On the next try, the new security alarm worked well and suffered no visible damage other than scorch marks from the exploding primer. Once I had it down pat, I churned out many of the altered mouse traps. We did not deploy any of them yet, but we had them ready if we ever did need them.

Amy had also downloaded simple plans to make similar trip wire alarms but using a loaded twelve gauge shotshell. That design used a piece of three-quarter inch iron pipe (which is apparently the perfect size to hold a twelve gauge shell) to act as a barrel for the shotshell. These would produce a loud report and could be aimed in any direction in which they could also be easily used to kill or wound an intruder. Obviously, these would be highly illegal now and should be used only in the direst of circumstances.

I did make one just to see if the design was viable or needed improvement. The one I made did seem to work and suffered no damage when I tried it out. But it was something we would never use unless the situation was really bad. Again Amy had bought all the needed supplies to make many of the twelve gauge traps.

She had bought several driveway alerts which would sound a chime if someone drove into the driveway. We tried one, and it worked fine if you walked in front of it too. They were battery powered, and of course, Amy had bought plenty of rechargeable batteries in the correct size. She also had purchased several battery chargers for different size batteries to cover all bases.

One of her plans was for me to alter the old clay pigeon thrower I had into something more lethal. I asked her what she had in mind, and she said maybe have it throw rocks or have it throw spears or something.

Well I like to make things, and I like a challenge, and I also had a lot of time on my hands now that I wasn't working. Making the thrower into a rock thrower would be easy enough, but the spear idea was more intriguing to me and more of a challenge.

I thought about the problem while staring at the old thrower. Then I walked around inside my workshop just looking around. I gathered up a few scraps and set to work. I worked all afternoon one day. But when I was done I was proud of what I had concocted. It was beautiful in a utilitarian way and worked fine, but I thought it was totally worthless.

I had cut some pieces of three eights inch rebar into short lengths. I could fit three of these into the small holders I had made for the thrower. After many tries, and I do mean many, I found the sweet spot and so the thrower would work well with the chunks of rebar. Of course, the chunks would not fly true at all. But I thought about how arrows are made with the feathers on them, and while I was not going to glue feathers on the rebar, I did tie short pieces of plastic trail tape to the rebar.

Now when you launched the rebar through the air, they flew pretty true with the bright colored trail tape streaming out behind. You could see them fly pretty easy now and they flew just fine. I made a dozen pieces of rebar the same size and sharpened one end of each. I sure would not want to get hit by one.

But still what was the point when we had many guns and plenty of ammunition? But it was fun to make, and it was fun to launch the rebar and watch it fly through the air and stick in the ground. I played for awhile trying different adjustments on the thrower to change the height they flew and such to see how to get the greatest range. I made Amy come out and watch me shoot it. She was suitably impressed and kissed me.

We still watched the news most evenings. There were riots almost continually now in many cities. Many, many more people were now on the food stamp program and they totally depended on that program for their food. The government was still supplying the same food stamp amount every month as before. The problem was that food prices had gone way up and selection had gone way down. The amount of value of the food stamps was not near enough for these people to live on anymore even if they were careful shoppers.

     Even the relatively low-cost staples like rice and ramen was a problem because much of it was imported and now they were not even available at any price. So the people rioted. And like many times in the past, the Governors of the states afflicted with rioting called out the state National Guard units to help keep the peace. Curfews were put in place in many cities. This helped but did not stop the underlying problem. That would take an act of Congress. And our Congress did not have a very good track record for passing anything.

Chapter 10

Even the larger city that was closest to us was having problems. It was not a major city, but still, the problem was the same. People depended on our government to keep them fed, and now they were unable to stretch the food stamps to feed them for a whole month. Of course, the local food pantries and churches were providing food to the needy, but they were soon overwhelmed, and their limited supply of food was exhausted.

There was a riot, and one of the grocery stores were looted and almost destroyed. That store was then boarded up, and it did not look like they planned to reopen. That was one less store for people to get food. Food became a major issue all across the nation.

Amy said she checked the internet just to see if she could order more food, even though we did not need any. Every website she tried had a notice that they were not accepting any new orders at this time. Two places she tried had pulled their websites and were not even active anymore. She just got a website not found notice. She said things would only get worse.

Then Congress did act. They rescinded the Posse Comitatus Act so the regular Army and other branches of the military could be used within our borders to keep the peace and enforce the laws inside the United States. This was mainly a symbolic gesture because since the John Warner National Defense Authorization Act for Fiscal Year 2007 the President already had the authorization to use the military inside the USA during an emergency. And the President decided if it was an emergency or not. I would think this current situation certainly qualified as an emergency.

So our military troops started to be recalled from posts all around the world and brought back to posts here inside the United States. This was a process and did not happen overnight, but it was put into motion. Most citizens saw this as a good thing. Many people didn't really like us spreading our troops all over the world anyway.

After this process of bringing home our troops was started, it was a major topic on the evening news for many days. Then the President issued a statement directed at all world leaders. Basically he said that we were indeed bringing most of our troops home and were even closing many of our military bases on foreign soil.

But at the same time, he reminded other countries that we really did not need military bases scattered all around the world to protect our nation. We could still strike anywhere in the world right from our bases on US soil. He made it very plain that if anyone thought they had a free hand now just because we were moving our troops they were mistaken. We were just as strong a military force as ever. And now everyone in the world knew he did not bluff.

Now military leaders were working with state Governors and even Mayors in the largest cities to move troops around to where they were needed to provide security for the cities. This would maybe help quell the violence at least for awhile but still did not fix the problem. We had Americans that went to bed hungry at night, and it looked like this situation would only get worse.

But it was not just the United States that was having trouble. It was almost worldwide. Every country was hurting even the third world countries. Every country did importing and exporting, and now that was just about stopped. At the same time, world tourism just about came to a stop. Out of, country credit cards would not work because there was no longer an exchange rate between different currencies. And any tourists would have to have local currency to do anything in a different country.

International airline flights just about totally stopped. Of course, the extreme fuel costs likely played a major role in this decision too. All world economies were in complete turmoil. International businesses just closed up totally or shank way down to just national companies. Most just went out of business.

Money deposited in foreign banks was a major problem for both individuals and businesses. In a few cases these banks gave back the money in the currency of the native country of the account, and they were happy to shed themselves of this foreign currency. But that only worked while they had enough of the proper currency on hand. Almost every bank refused to give out local currency to foreign depositors. And those depositors did not want any of that foreign currency anyway. So there was an impasse.

People of the world were facing an interesting problem. They all had money that worked where they lived, but it had virtually no value when they left their own country. Inflation was running rampant in all countries and that of course included the United States.

With inflation going up so fast wages could not keep up, and many businesses were failing. With the high inflation retailers would sell their product for a profit but when they went to reorder the new wholesale price would be higher than the price they had sold their products for. It gave them a net loss when they reordered. They would buy an item for five dollars and sell it for nine dollars and then when they reordered they would have to pay thirteen dollars for the same item.

And if they did reorder they might find that item would no longer sell because their customers could no longer afford it. It was ruining many retailers, and they were folding up at a record pace. Of course whenever any business would close all their employees would be out of work. People out of work could not afford to buy near as much, and that would make it hard for other retailers. Then they would go out of business and the cycle would continue and expand.

So many people were on unemployment and found their financial situation untenable. On unemployment, they get about seventy-five percent of their wages as unemployment benefits. So if they had been making one hundred dollars, they now would be getting seventy-five dollars. And at the same time inflation was going way up, so they needed more money than they were making just to make ends meet. They just couldn't survive on the unemployment. Their only possible option to survive was to steal.

Things were so bad that more and more people would break the law just to get arrested so they would be fed three meals a day and have a place to sleep. This, of course, caused other problems.

Before this, all started most cities, counties, and states were having budget problems. Cities were filing for bankruptcy, and a couple of the states were in dire financial trouble. And then this mess happened that only made the problems bigger.

People ran out of money, they lost their jobs, and could hardly even afford enough food to eat. Sales tax revenue fell for all levels of government. With super high fuel prices, there was no travel or tourism. This meant less tax revenue. Fuel consumption dropped dramatically, so fuel tax revenues dropped to record low levels.

Income dropped, so people were not paying income taxes. Many people who owned homes and businesses could not afford to pay their property taxes. Businesses closed so they did not pay their business taxes. There was no new building happening, so no one was paying for building permits.

Overall tax revenues across the board dropped way down. At the same time, there were increases in needed services provided by all levels of government. So cuts had to be made. There were many layoffs at all levels of government below the national level. Of course, many of those getting laid off were old enough, so they took retirement instead. This put a big strain on all the pension plans.

The pensions were almost all way underfunded long before this event happened. Then when this started the stock markets, all fell dramatically, so these pension funds were hurt badly. Now everyone that could was retiring, with many even taking very early retirement. The pension funds just did not have enough money. So there were no choices to be made because there was only one option available. And that was to cut benefits to all pensioners. And in almost all cases this meant massive cuts to benefits no matter how many people it hurt.

Chapter 11

Amy was being proved right of course. We like many other people in the United States would likely be losing our retirement funds. All the big banks were in big trouble. Like anyone in the stock market, the banks had lost a bundle. And maybe it was worse for the banks because many were invested abroad and lost all that money also.

And then there were all the mortgages that were delinquent. People just did not have enough money to make mortgage payments. People that did have money in savings accounts or in other bank accounts withdrew all that money, just like Amy and I had done. At least some people got to withdraw their money from the banks.

The early bird gets the worm, and the early birds got their deposits out of the banks before the banks stopped allowing withdrawals. All the big banks closed for 'reorganization.' There was no money. Banks had leveraged their money many times, too many times. Now they were all broke. Way beyond being broke. They had fallen so far down the well that they could not even see the light at the top.

So it was with the FDIC, the mighty Federal Deposit Insurance Corporation. That turned out to be a joke, and the joke was on all the depositors of the banks. The FDIC only had a fraction of the money needed to pay off all the depositors. Congress could give the FDIC more money of course. The Federal government had unlimited money because they could just print more. But Congress hesitated. They thought about it but did nothing. Amy said there was just no point now. Things were past the point of no return.

And our retirement accounts were in one of the big banks. Now that money was just gone. It would not be coming back. I kissed Amy and thanked her for saving most of our wealth. We had turned most of our money, which was becoming more worthless every day, into tangible goods. Stuff we could use or eat or trade. All thanks to Amy acting fast when speed was required.

We were fine right now, but we were the exception in the nation and in the world. People everywhere were starving, even in the once great United States of America. Europe was a mess. People were killing each other over there. And many were starving over there. But it was the same most places.

Things would reset. Things would get better. But first things had to get bad enough to hit rock bottom, so the only way to go was up. Only then could the slow road to recovery happen. And though things were bad now, we were still a long way away from the bottom yet. Many people were going to die all around the world.

The first war started in the Middle East which should not have been a surprise to anyone. They had been at war over there for centuries. The thing that was a surprise was that no one attacked Israel. Israel was an island of peace while fighting was going on all around them.

Maybe there was a tiny spark of intelligence in some of those countries. I assume they knew that Israel was sitting there with their collective fingers on the trigger of many nukes and I think most everyone knew that Israel would use those nukes if they thought they needed to do so to save their people.

So the Middle East was in flames with bombs and missiles flying around. America, Russia, and China were all holed up in their respective countries and did not get involved.

Next, there were many localized wars here and there on the African continent. Again none of the three superpowers got involved. China's only foreign base was there, but even the Africans were smart enough to stay away from that base.

Then stupid North Korea where all of this really started made a move. They attacked South Korea and Japan. But they were stupid and had not been careful enough because the United States was watching everything they were doing every single day.

North Korea attacked, and it later seemed that we must have had missiles and aircraft in the air before the first shot was ever fired by North Korea. South Korea took a big hit, and many died. But then a large wave of cruise missiles hit North Korea.

So far there were only conventional weapons used by either side. Then the Norks made their second mistake. They launched nukes at both South Korea and Japan. South Korea with the America's help shot down those incoming missiles. Japan was not quite so lucky, and one nuclear armed missile made it through all their defenses and detonated.

Then three missiles were launched at North Korea from the ocean not very far from the Korean Peninsula. These three missiles contained multiple independently targetable reentry vehicles. The three missiles became twenty-four nuclear warheads that struck twenty-four different locations within North Korea. At that point for all intents and purposes North Korea ceased to exist.

There was still ground fighting, and that continued for over a week before it mostly died out. South Korea took a terrible beating, and millions of lives were lost. Japan had also taken many, many casualties. But that war was over, and it would not be repeated. North Korea would never be a country again.

Russia and China did nothing. They had enough problems within their own countries. Russia was in better shape of the two. China was being torn up from within. They would just have to sort that out on their own. Russia was used to hard times, and they would get by. It was a big country with many natural resources. And the people there were hardy, and hardships were just part of their lives. There was talk that Russia was deporting all Muslims from their country but this was never verified.

Pakistan and India were scrapping along their joint border as they had done for many years. There was much talk about the clash becoming a nuclear war between the two. India was suffering more from world economic troubles than Pakistan, but both were having troubles, and many thought nukes would soon be flying through the air between the two countries.

Surprisingly China put a stop to that talk. China said it would destroy both countries and occupy both if their squabble turned nuclear. That seemed to do the trick, and no nuclear missiles were fired by either side. Everyone knew it could still flare up but it had calmed down for the present anyway.

So many countries were having catastrophic problems, and most were looking for somewhere to vent their anger. But other than localized clashes and the ongoing war in the Middle East things quieted down and World War Three was put on hold for another time.

Countries turned and looked inside their borders instead and tried to fix the unfixable. Most had never faced anything like this in their history. The countries of the world had tied their collective economies so tightly together that now all were in great turmoil.

Many multinational talks were ongoing trying to come up with an agreed upon currency or some medium of exchange that could be used between all countries. There was some very limited trade started up between a few countries, but it was more barter and fiat currencies were not being used. Sometimes it was an agreed upon amount of gold traded for an agreed upon amount of goods, but it was all on a very limited scale. All the world's fiat currencies were dead outside of each country's own borders.

The world of debt had now collapsed. There were thousands of grievances lodged in the world court consisting mostly of non-payments. In almost every case it boiled down to the massive debt that each country and the multitude of international banks had built up. There had never been enough money or value in the entire world to cover all the debt. Let alone the derivatives market which was well over a quadrillion.

There was no answer. They talked about debt on the news, but there really was little to talk about. Who really thought that the United States would ever pay off the twenty-two trillion dollars of national debt? And it was the same in almost every other country. There was just too much debt.

The debt had forced the collapse, not our current President. It had to come at some point. He just was the trigger. Sure we could have made it another year or even maybe a few years, but the collapse of world debt had to happen at some point. And now the world was left to try and pick up the pieces. And the world population would suffer greatly. Suffer like never before.

Chapter 12

Here in America, the military was trying to keep order and maintain the peace. But people were starving. There was an exodus from many of the large cities. People just left in search of greener pastures or at least some food. They left by car or bus or bicycle, or they walked.

This mass was like locusts, and they engulfed much of what they encountered. Smaller towns did not stand a chance against the mass of starving people. Thousands died. People tried to protect what was theirs by any means they could, which most often involved firearms. Sometimes streets were littered with bodies. But still, the mass was pushed forward by those behind. They would step over and stumble on the dead bodies of those who went first but still they continued forward.

Towns tried to seal themselves off and it was relatively easy to stop vehicular traffic from entering in many cases. But on foot, the mass just surged around and over any barriers that were erected to stop them. In at least two cases forests were set on fire between small towns and the encroaching horde. The fire itself posed no threat but the smoke killed countless from smoke inhalation, and the thick smoke worked to stop the mass from advancing.

But even this extreme method was only a stop-gap solution. The fires would only last for so long then the smoke would dissipate, and the masses would again surge forward. Often times, residents of the small towns were left with nothing, and many then joined the ranks of the invading army that had decimated everything in these overrun towns.

While the evacuating masses of people could overwhelm any small town and single residence that they encountered and steal any food they found, it was never enough. The roads were soon littered with the dead and the dying. Those trying to flee were hampered by the high cost of fuel and the availability of fuel. With the banks closed, no credit cards could be used. No debit cards worked and that included the EBT cards used for food stamps.

Places that still had food would only accept cash, and the prices were extremely high. Even with police and military protection stores were looted of everything. Truckers refused to deliver because most trucks were hijacked which almost always meant the death of the driver.

The only recourse was convoys with fully armed military escorts. This only led to many more deaths. In the eastern states where towns and cities were closer together, people could walk in search of food. In the western states where even small towns might be tens of miles apart walking was not a viable option. Of course, desperate people tried it and died as the result.

Some died from starvation or exhaustion while others died from dysentery from drinking surface water from creeks, ponds, and lakes. The population of the United States was dropping and at a rapid pace that was still accelerating.

All livestock was at risk. When people are starving, they will eat most anything. Cows, horses, pigs, goats, chickens, cats, dogs, and any other creature that could be caught and killed was eaten by the starving people. Even crops in the fields were stripped and eaten, whether ripe or not.

Those that had guns would shoot, kill, and eat any wild bird or animal they could find. This included anything from mice and songbirds on up to larger birds and animals. Thousands of people that had never fished in their lives were trying it now with all manner of home-made fishing equipment.

In the Eastern states with higher human population densities, wild fish and game populations were decimated until only the smartest, and wariest wild animal survived. The sad part was the destruction of all the livestock with much of the meat going to waste with spoilage and none left for reproduction.

In the west where there were large numbers of game animals and much smaller, human populations things were better. In western America, with the distances so vast and the limited roads, the game populations did not suffer as much as in the eastern states. When hunting pressure increased, the big game populations retreated back into much more rugged areas where hunting was at best difficult and at worst deadly for the hunters.

Even on our property well out away from any big city, we sometimes would now hear shots from hunters. We realized that even where we lived, it was no longer a totally safe haven. I set up many of the non-lethal alarms around the place. Guns were loaded and left in handy spots around the house.

Both Amy and I took to carrying a handgun all the time. We had no livestock, so we did not have to worry about trying to protect them. We both wondered about the shots we heard and whether the shots led to dead deer and elk or to dead beef cattle or even dead horses. We tried not to think that the shots maybe meant dead people.

The first time one of our primer alarms went off, all we saw was a very scared young elk running for all it was worth away from what scared it. It gave us a chuckle and showed us that the alarm worked and that we had no trouble hearing it even inside the house. That one was in the middle of the day. The second time we heard an alarm, it was at night, and I grabbed one of the AR rifles and flipped on all the exterior lights.

This time it was a man and between the bang of the alarm and the explosion of lights, he was already running away. I did not hesitate a second and I shot a half a dozen rounds in his general direction but not close enough so I would hit him by accident. I realized two things right then and there. One was that we made a tactical mistake by not having any rifle sights that would be functional at night and that next time there was a good chance I would have to shoot to kill.

I never bothered going back to bed, and neither did Amy. We stayed up the rest of the night and drank coffee and talked. I told her that there was about a hundred percent chance that person was up to no good. He had been carrying something in one hand, but I could not quite make out what it was for sure in the near darkness. My guess was that it was crowbar, but it could have been a gun.

"We are going to have to shoot someone sooner or later. I don't think people will just leave us alone."

"You really think it will come to that?"

"Yes, I do now. I did think we would never even see anyone, but now I think different. There was no reason for that man to come here in the middle of the night. If he needed emergency help, he would not have run away. He ran because he was up to no good. That is the only explanation. Next time the intruder might fight back rather than run away."

"I don't want to shoot anyone."

"Neither do I but I will kill a thousand to protect you if necessary."

We talked more until the east started to lighten up. Then we made breakfast together, and afterward together we put up more of the primer alarm traps. Also close to the house we put a couple of the electronic driveway alarms. While setting them up, I did the work while Amy kept watch. Next, I redirected some of our exterior lights to give us better coverage. I also ran wires to some of the lights so I could add additional lights off the same switch. Next time there would be much better lighting shining out but leaving me in the shadows.

When done with that I worked in the shop and made several more of the lethal shotgun alarms. I hoped this was just wasted time, but I felt that was not the case. The intruder last night had me spooked. I felt he would be back. And likely not alone. I vowed that I would be better prepared for our next go-round.

Chapter 13

In the afternoon I made Amy stay inside while I took a rifle and made a big circuit around the place. I was looking for where anyone might have been watching the house or any tracks. I think I was relieved when I found no such place, but then I wondered if I just missed it. I knew it would be very easy for someone to sneak up to within a couple of hundred yards of the house and wait under cover and shoot us when we came outside. The bad part was that I could do nothing to prevent that from happening, other than just stay inside all the time.

We were even weaker at night when anyone could walk up close, and we would never be able to see them. Our only defense was all the trip wire alarms we now had deployed. That guy that set off the one last night would know about those alarms now and be more careful. The driveway alarms were only placed near the house. If one of those went off, it meant we were in real trouble and the bad guys would be very close.

That night it was quiet, which was a good thing because both Amy and I were tired because we'd missed so much sleep the night before. But we woke refreshed and after breakfast, I went out to my shop and made some more of the twelve gauge lethal alarms. I had a different plan for these.

Like many women, Amy had various decorations placed up around the house. And some of them would be perfect for what I wanted. I did exchange a couple of her display pieces, but for the most part, I just moved them temporarily while I was working and then put them back where they were, to begin with.

Amy watched me work after I explained exactly what I was doing and why. When I was all done, I cut the ends from enough shotgun shells so I could test all the new alarms I had just put out. I cut the ends off the ammo so I could remove the shot and all of the powder, so there was just the primed case left. That would be perfect just for this test.

I tried all the home-made lethal alarms, and they functioned as I expected. I reloaded all of them with regular buckshot. These were now very lethal, and I hoped never to use them. They were hidden behind the decorations that Amy had always had near the house. I had securely fastened the traps to the house with each of the barrels pointed slightly out from the wall.

When fired they would spray deadly buckshot down alongside the house. Anyone standing near the house would be hit. Maybe they wouldn't be killed but it was very likely they would be hit. Instead of normal trip wires to make them go off, I just brought the trigger wires along the edge of the house where they were hard to see and through the doorway into the house. These would be set off with a sharp pull from inside when the time was right.

By the time I was all done the day was about used up. I grilled venison steaks on the gas grill for us for supper. We both retired early to bed as was our normal custom. Sleep came easily, but both of us were jolted awake when one of the driveway alarms chimed in our bedroom during the night.

We both leaped out of bed. I hesitated only long enough to slip on a pair of pants before I ran downstairs. I snatched up one of the AR rifles and carefully made my way near one of the windows.

The driveway alarm worked very well and was only loud enough to wake us and not be heard by anyone outside. Neither Amy nor I had turned on a light. Whoever was out there had no idea we had been alerted. Now near a window, I just listened.

I heard Amy come quietly down the stairs. I heard her pick up the other rifle like I had in my hands. Then she made no more noise, so I assumed she was standing still. That's when I heard the whispering just on the other side of the window.

"Do you see anything?"

"No, it's dark in there."

"I can't wait to have some time with that woman. You were right; she sure is a looker. I bet they have a bunch of food in there too."

"How do you want to do this?"

"I don't see a reason for us to split up. I say we just bust in through the door with guns ready."

I had heard enough, and I moved quietly to the front door. When I started to move, I realized Amy had snuck over near me without me even being aware of her. She followed me noiselessly.

At the front door, I waited for just a moment until Amy was ready. I pointed at the exterior light switches and at her. Then I pointed at me and the strings by the door. When I saw she was ready, I pulled two of the strings hard and then I opened the front door. The strings led to two of the twelve gauge alarms and they both roared when I pulled the strings. These were on the side where I had heard the men talking.

On cue with the roar of the twelve gauge shells going off, Amy switched on the outside lights. As I stepped through the doorway I saw one man standing and fired two or three times from the hip at him. He went down and then I saw the second man on the ground.

Then I raised the rifle to my shoulder and shot into each body twice, so there was no chance they were alive and just playing possum. I pivoted back and forth looking for more threats, but I saw no one else around anywhere.

I held up my hand so Amy knew I wanted her to stay put just inside the doorway and I made a quick circuit around the house. I saw no one else anywhere.

With the outside lights on there was plenty of light so I made a quick check of the two dead bodies and I grabbed their guns after I was sure they were indeed dead. Then I went back inside and shut the door and shut off the outside lights and set the guns down.

Amy came into my arms and was crying. I just held her and let her cry it out. When she stopped all she said was that she heard what they said. Again sleep was out of the question for both of us, and we moved to the couch and sat there together holding each other. We were still in the same position when it started to get lighter outside. Neither of us wanted any food, so I just made us coffee for breakfast.

After we had each finished a cup, I went up and got fully dressed. Then I left Amy inside, and I went out to haul away the garbage. I got my truck and a rope and tied one end of the rope to the feet of each man. Then I backed my truck up close enough so I could loop the rope over the ball hitch. Before I dragged them off, I went through their pockets and took what they had with them. Then I just drove out the driveway and down the gravel road for more than a mile.

I then stopped and untied the slip knots in the rope and rolled the bodies into the ditch. Work done, I drove back home and put the truck away. Next, I hosed down the area where the bodies fell until you could see no traces of the puddles of blood. I also sprayed down the bloody drag marks as far as the hose would reach. When I was done I went inside and washed up.

I felt nothing for the trash I had killed. When I heard what they said about Amy I knew only that I wanted to kill them. Not chase them off or wound them but kill them dead. And now I did not feel bad or sad or anything else. I was actually glad. I was glad they were dead and that Amy was safe. I knew now that I would kill any man or beast that threatened my Amy. I knew I would not freeze up. And I knew I would not hesitate.

Chapter 14

The next several days passed uneventfully. Every couple days I would hike completely around the place to look for signs of more possible intruders. It had been a few days now since we had heard any shots in the distance. Maybe we were now alone. But I would not bet on it.

The weather was cooling off, and fall was certainly in the air. Amy's garden was all done, and the fruit trees were also done. There had been much more fruit this year, and we had dried, canned, and froze the excess that we did not eat fresh. Deer and elk could not get through the high fence, but they could certainly smell the fruit, and it drew them in close.

When I saw an elk one morning, I decided it was time for us to take one for meat. Though I could have used my regular hunting rifle, I decided to try out that big Barrett fifty caliber. It was just as well because by the time I had got the rifle, the elk had wandered back away some. I guessed he was at about three hundred yards. It would have been a shot I would have taken with my regular rifle and should be no problem at all for the Barrett.

I got set up and then watched the elk through the scope waiting for the right moment to squeeze the trigger. When the elk turned mostly broadside to me and paused I squeezed off the shot. The heavy slug did its work, and the elk hit the ground like he had been hit with a big hammer. I watched through the scope for several minutes, but I saw no movement. Amy had followed me out when I went in to get the rifle.

"I guess that worked."

"I guess it did."

I saw no reason to wait or to work hard, so I got my truck and a couple of items and drove out to the elk. It was very dead. I gutted it right there and used a come-a-long that I hooked to the front of the pickup box to pull the elk up the loading ramp I had brought with me. I never worked up a sweat, and I soon had the elk in the back of the pickup.

I backed into the big shed and attached the gambrel to the elk's hind legs. I hoisted it up right from the back of the truck, so it would be handy for skinning. The rest of the day was spent cutting the meat up, soaking it in jerky spices, and then putting the slices in the big smoker. All of the elk could not be done that day, but it was cold enough, so there was no hurry. We had elk tenderloin for the evening meal. And a fine meal it was too.

It took three days to process all the elk meat. With a good portion in jerky and the rest wrapped and frozen. I looked in the freezer after we were done and saw we had plenty of room in there yet. I would be shooting a second elk unless Amy beat me to it.

We had our first snowfall. It was only an inch or less, and it melted the same day, but it was a start. This year for the first time I was looking forward to a snowy winter. It would seal us off from the rest of the world and help keep us safe.

Amy did shoot an elk. It was a spike bull, so it was almost guaranteed to be good eating. Most of that one was put in the freezer though we did smoke and turn some into more jerky. This time it was a different jerky/spice recipe which both of us liked better. We had found our new standard for jerky for next year.

When we did get snow, and it stayed, I pulled all the alarms and traps we had set out. I did this before the snow got very deep at all to make it easier for me. It was going to be a long winter. The TV stations had all gone off the air. Well, that's not quite right. All the regular stations did go off the air, but there were three replacements.

All were produced by the government. One was strictly news and weather that was repeated again and again throughout the day and night with random updates. Another was an information channel, kind of like youtube, only a little more, clinical you might say. It showed how-to videos all day long on many different things.

Like how to make candles from different things like cooking oil or Crisco. Or different ways to help keep warm in the winter. Several ways to start fires without matches. Herbs and other items that could be used to ease the loss of prescription medicines. How to fish through the ice. How to clean and cook fish. Cleaning and cooking pigeons and squirrels. They had quite a few different videos, and all of them were designed to help keep more of the population alive.

We watched many of the videos over winter. While not the intent, some were funny. The third channel the government showed was twenty-fours a day of old TV shows. Some were old enough to be in black and white, and none were newer than the seventy's with most being older. We even watched some of them just for the nostalgia of seeing them and to just pass the time.

There was only one radio station broadcasting. It was just the audio of the government news TV channel. Just news and weather. The news now was way different than what the old evening TV news shows were like. It was just a guy or a woman reading a script. There were no video feeds or on the scene reporting, just strict matter-of-fact reports. And it was the government, so both Amy and I questioned the honesty of what was reported. But it was the only game in town so-to-speak, so we watched it, usually twice a day to catch any updates.

The weather reports were similar to the old news shows. Radar of weather patterns, warnings of predicted snowfall or high winds. No video of any cities getting plowed out or anything like that. There was never any video of any city on either the news or weather. And that part was rather worrisome. There was no internet anymore, and our cell phones had no signal. Our landline house phone had no dial tone either. So our one and only source of news and information were the government broadcast channels on TV or radio.

I was right the winter was a long one. Well okay, it was a regular winter, but it just seemed longer. Our county road past our house was never plowed once all winter. It was impassable for over three months. Not that either of us really cared. No travel meant we were safe here.

Both Amy and I wondered just how many people died over winter. It must have been a very large number but we never really discussed it, and it certainly was never on the government news channel. Even where we lived in the country, I bet many died. Thanks to Amy we had plenty of food here, both food we bought and what we grew or killed here. But what about the other people around here? They certainly could not go to town during the winter for supplies. And what if they were on some medications that could not be refilled all winter? And what about heat if they did not have a wood stove?

We burned wood mostly for heat all winter. We even used the wood stove to cook some of our meals, all to save on the propane. We had plenty of propane, but we had no idea when more could be purchased and delivered. We did not know if the electric power was on for other people or not. We were totally off the grid here, so we had electric power but did not know about everyone else. Of course on the news, they never mentioned the electrical power status for anywhere in the country. Obviously, some places had bad storms during the winter that would have taken down power lines. Were those electric lines repaired right away? Or even repaired at all?

Again there was no way for us to know. In snowy areas, if the power lines were damaged then the roads would have to be plowed to allow the repair trucks to go out and fix the power. Was that done? With no phone service, how would people let the power company know the power was out? Though we didn't know if other parts of the country had phone service or not. We only knew we did not have any phone service.

      Both Amy and I thought it would have been nice to have the capability to at least listen to shortwave and ham radio broadcasts. But it was too late for that now. I even wondered if the government would let radio operators talk freely anymore. I imagine that it would be relatively easy for our military to jam the radio waves. I'm sure we must have that technology.

Chapter 15

When spring finally came, there was plenty of work for us to do. And we were both anxious to start it. When things were warm enough, I worked up Amy's garden plot the same as always. She had plenty of seeds to plant so that would not be a problem. We had saved some potatoes over winter, and though they looked pretty bad to me, Amy assured me that they would likely grow fine. She's the expert, not me on the garden stuff.

After some discussion, we decided to drive into the closest small town. Both of us wanted real news and information. And if possible we wanted to buy a few fresh foods if they were available. We both went armed. Amy was legally armed because she still had a valid permit and I was illegally armed with a handgun. We also had the two AR rifles in the truck, but those were unloaded and cased so they should be perfectly legal to carry that way. We did have loaded magazines ready, so it would only take moments to uncase and load the rifles. We had no idea what to expect.

It was rather eerie driving in. There was no traffic of any kind. The gravel road showed no signs of travel at all. We drove past several places, and none showed any signs of life. Of course, there could have been people living in them but we did not see anyone, and none of the driveways showed any fresh tire tracks that we noticed.

It was the same all way to the small town. The town had around fifteen hundred population I think at the last census, but it didn't look like that now. It was like a ghost town. No one was driving anywhere, and we saw no one walking around.

"Drive to the grocery store. If someone is here, that's where they would be."

So I drove to the grocery store, and there were several vehicles in the parking lot. Actually there were quite a few vehicles, which surprised both of us. Lots of cars and trucks but we still saw no people. I parked, and we just sat in my truck for a little bit. Still nothing so we got out.

With no place else to go we walked up toward the front door. Just before we got to the door, it happened.

"You all aren't planning to bust in are yuh?"

I think both of us jumped a foot off the ground. We both turned, and there was an old man sitting in a lawn chair between some outside displays. We had both missed seeing him there before he spoke. He had a rifle lying across his lap.

"No, we had no intention of breaking in. Actually we had hoped things were better and we could buy some fresh food. Where is everyone?"

"Read the poster on the door, and then ya'll come over, and we'll talk."

So that is what we did. We walked to the front doors, and there was indeed a posting there. It was from FEMA. It was dated November seventeenth, several months ago. Basically it just said that FEMA had set up many aid stations and emergency centers all across America. Any citizen was welcome at any of these FEMA shelters where they would be given food, medical treatment, and housing as needed.

These shelters were scattered across the nation, and the closest one was in the nearest larger city from here. Directions were given on the poster, and it also stated that on November thirtieth the military would return here and offer free transportation to the nearest shelter.

Anyone wishing to take advantage of this free transportation was to meet at this location by one in the afternoon on November thirtieth. This offer was for not just residents of this town but also for anyone in the surrounding area.

Citizens were told only to bring one bag per person that contained just clothing, toiletries, and any prescription medications they required. All other needs would be provided by the government at the shelters. Anyone going to the shelters was free to come and go as they pleased and free return transportation would be arranged in the near future for those who wished to return to this particular location.

It seemed pretty straight forward and reasonable. It would be far easier to have people together to easier feed them and provide warm accommodations. We walked over to the old man.

"So the whole town left to go to the shelter?"

"Yep. Pretty much every person from town and many from the surrounding area. Some drove themselves, and some rode in the military trucks and the obviously commandeered school buses."

"So what did the people think about the place when they came back here?"

"That's just it. No one ever came back. Not one out of all the people. And many had their own rigs to drive."

"So did the military ever come back again to pick up anyone who missed the first load?"

"Nope. Matter of fact I never saw any traffic at all until you two just showed up here. You two are the first people I have seen since Walter died from what I think was a heart attack in January."

"The shelters must be pretty nice for nobody to come back to their homes."

The old man let out a snort.

"Yeah, I bet they're really nice and cozy. Like the dome, people went to during the Katrina hurricane fiasco."

"But the conditions in that dome were horrible. Everyone from here would have returned if conditions were like that at this shelter."

"Yep, you'd certainly think so wouldn't ya. But not a single person came back for any reason. You tell me, what are the odds of everyone wanting to stay even if it was so wonderful?"

"You're right. You can never have everyone happy. Some would have come back here. If for nothing else just to brag about it."

"You got that right. The only reason nobody came back was that they couldn't."

"You mean held there against their will? I don't think our President would stand for that. He seemed like a straight shooter."

"Oh, you must mean the elected President."

"Who else would I be talking about?"

"The real President and the Vice President died. The Speaker of the House was the next in line, and he is now acting President."

"What happened to our President?"

"That's the hundred dollar question now, isn't it? They said he died and that's it. End of story. Now we are blessed with this new guy."

"I kind of always thought the Speaker was kind of a weasel."

"I would be careful who you said that to iffin' I was you."

"This is still America!"

"Is it? It doesn't say it on that poster, but the whole country is under Martial Law now. It happened right after we got our brand new President. Imagine that."

"I can hardly believe all this."

"I don't care if you believe me or not. Why don't you and your pretty misses just hop in your old truck and drive over to that there special shelter in the city. I bet they would take you in with open arms. Then just drive back here later and tell me again how wrong I am."

"Let me rephrase my last statement. I don't want to believe any of this."

"That is much better. I see you are packin'. You think they would let anyone in the shelter have a gun? Or a knife or likely even a spoon?"

"Okay, I get it. And we have no intention of driving to the city. What about you? Why didn't you go to the shelter with everyone else? Surely you had friends go there."

"I just have always had a hard time believing most anything the government ever said ever since Vietnam. I sure wasn't going to someplace where they were in complete control.

"But besides putting up the poster, the military hung around here for an hour or more talking to the people here when they dropped off the poster. Told how wonderful the shelter was and everything. Anyone with even half a brain knew that couldn't be true.

"When the military came back to haul the people to the shelter, there was more of 'em, and they were all armed. I was nearby, but I stayed well back out of sight and just watched what was going on. Everyone had their bags searched before they could get on a bus. It looked like a lot of stuff was taken away from them. Arguments were dealt with rather harshly. The military had trash cans that they threw people's possessions into as the troopers searched all the bags.

"When they all left some of the trash cans, the military took with them and some they just left in the parking lot. I assume the ones they took had things of some value. The ones they left had things like photo albums, knick-knacks, and other things that had no real monetary value. The cans left here I put in a nearby garage to keep them out of the weather."

"Sure doesn't sound like America to me."

"Sure don't. But it is what it is."

"So now you just sit here waiting for something?"

"Yep. I'm waiting to die. My meds ran out about a month ago or more. And that's alright. I'm too old for a revolution anyway, and I wouldn't stand to be herded into some concentration camp. If they come back, I'll fight until I die. Not likely to take long when the time comes."

Chapter 16

There was little to do but go home again. We bid the old man goodbye after a little more talk. He did not seem sad but just seemed resigned to his fate. Amy and I were mostly silent on the ride back home. When we got to the turnoff from the asphalt road to our gravel county road, she had me stop and asked if we should cut some brush to drag behind the truck to disguise our truck tracks on the gravel road.

I thought it likely wasn't necessary but did as she asked. I also tried to drive on the tracks I had left when we had driven earlier so everything would be brushed out. Two days later it rained some anyway and that likely erased any trace of our travel.

I was upset about what we learned from the old man. It was only after we got home that either of us realized that we had never traded names. Amy thought that the old man had not given us his name on purpose and that it was just as well that we remained nameless as well.

But I was constantly pacing the floor and thinking about what we had learned. Amy cautioned me that we had only received the information from one source and it could be all bogus. I asked her if she thought it was bogus and she admitted that it seemed true and the old man seemed to be telling the truth, and he seemed to be of sound mind. And most telling was that he seemed sad because it was true.

I wanted to do something. If this was true, it was time for a rebellion. I wanted to fight to get my country back. Amy did not. She asked me what exactly did I plan on doing? Where exactly would I go? Who exactly would I fight?

I told her that my first stop would be the so-called shelter in the city. It was relatively close, and they had printed out the directions so I would have no trouble finding it. She asked me if I thought they wouldn't have troops watching the roads leading to the city, to catch people coming in or trying to flee?

Even if I made it into the city for their shelter to work, they would have to have control over the whole city. For that, at a minimum they would need many roving patrols throughout the city and likely the surrounding area. And exactly how would I know about the patrols and how exactly would I avoid them?

"Okay. I don't have a plan, but I want to go and do something."

"Well, it seems logical to remain here until you do have a plan before we go off half-cocked."

"What do you mean 'we'?"

"Do you really think you could leave and I would just remain here? If you leave here, it will not be alone."

"But I would not want you to go."

"Exactly the same way I feel but what, it's different because you are a man? Do you really want to say that?"

I was just silent for a bit.

"I think I should just stay here and try to come up with a plan."

"Smart man. That's why I married you. We will stay here, and if the situation changes then together, we will deal with it."

So that was that. With spring here there were things to do anyway. We still had plenty of food, but the garden crop would be very important for our survival. As soon as Amy thought it was warm enough we worked together to plant the big garden. I had done some pruning on the fruit trees just before winter, and now I hauled that debris away from the orchard.

When we had caught up with things around the place Amy agreed to stay home, and I hiked to a couple of the neighbors to check on them. I approached the first place very carefully. I watched from a distance for a time before I advanced on the house. I decided to just walk right up the driveway in the hopes they would recognize me, and I wouldn't get shot.

When I got close enough, I called out. There was no answer, and I called out louder. Still, no response, so I walked up to the house. Everything looked normal with no bullet holes or busted windows on the house. I knocked on the door and yelled, but still, there was no answer. I tried the door and it opened, but I shut it again for now. I decided to check the barn first.

I yelled out before I opened the barn door but by this time I expected no answer. It stunk in the barn and not from just manure either. There were two long-dead horses in stalls in the barn. Now I guessed what I would find in the house.

Back at the house I walked inside and called out, but the smell told me there would be no answer. I found Betty dead in one bedroom. She had been naked when she was shot. It had obviously happened quite some time back. I found a clean sheet and covered the body. I looked through the whole house, but I could not find Frank. Cupboards in the kitchen were standing open. For now, I never looked in them.

Not finding Frank in the house I started searching around outside. I found him next to one of the outbuildings. Well, I cannot honestly say for sure that it was Frank, but I think what I found had been Frank. I found an old tarp and wrapped up what I did find of him.

Back at the house, I looked around some more. In two of the bedrooms, there were large backpacks. The beds were unmade and not too clean. Betty would never have let them be in that kind of shape. I went through the backpacks. Each contained similar items. Men's clothing, a few items of food, odds, and ends, ammunition, jewelry, one had a wad of cash and the other some silver coins and one gold coin.

    Rightly or wrongly I guessed that the two packs had been the property of the two men I had killed. I took the cash, the precious metal coins, and the ammunition with me when I left. But before I did leave I was able to start one of Frank's tractors and dug a hole with the bucket near the edge of the trees that surrounded the place. I then carefully laid the wrapped bodies of Frank and Betty in the hole and pushed the dirt back over them.

    Later I would make a point of coming back and putting up a cross with their names on it to mark their gravesite. I went back home before going to any other neighbors today. At home, I told Amy what I had found and what I had done there. I did not know the neighbors all that well, but Amy knew them better. She cried in my arms for some time before drying her eyes.

    "The power is out."

    Amy looked at me in surprise at my outburst.

    "What are you talking about?"

    "Frank and Betty's house. The power must be off because the house would be a real mess if the power was still on. The pump would still be working, and the house would be a flooded mess."

    "What does the pump have to do with it?"

    "They have been dead a long time, likely since I shot those two before snowfall. Things in the house would have frozen solid over winter and burst the water pipes. Now in the warm weather, the pipes would have thawed out and if the pump was still pumping the whole house would have been dripping water from all the burst pipes. So the power must be out and has likely been out for a long time. I have to go back there and turn off the main breaker, so when the power comes back on again, the pump will not start pumping water to flood the house."

"Okay, I understand. Yes, you should go and do that before the power returns. The power might come back on today or maybe ten years from now."

"Either way it would be a shame for the house to be ruined from leaking water pipes. I should check on the other neighbors too."

"Tomorrow is soon enough for both."

Chapter 17

So the next morning I walked back to Frank's place and shut off the main breaker. I also did a walk-through of the house just looking it over. There was only one bathroom, and the toilet had frozen and broke. There was little food in the cupboards, but I just left it there. I did tidy up just a little in the house before I left.

I did a quick walk-through of the barn and sheds just to see what was in them. Just for future reference in case, we needed to borrow something. When I was done I left and headed for the next neighbor. I had a bad feeling about what I would find there because they were on the town side and the bad guys would likely have stopped there first.

When I got to the other neighbor's house, I again announced myself loudly. Again there was no reply, and I didn't expect one. I knocked on the house door, and when there was no answer, I tried the door. It was unlocked, and I entered after again calling out. This house did not stink inside. A pleasant surprise. I walked through the house and entered each room.

There were no dead bodies. I think the owners had left on their own. I ran out and checked the garage, and one truck was gone. Back inside the house, I did notice that the cupboards were all again standing open. I checked the back door, and I could see that it had been broken into. My guess was by the same two guys. Good thing the owners were gone.

I did shut the main breaker off, but I think the owners had drained the water before they left. Nothing seemed to be broken from being frozen over winter. There must have been a separate switch somewhere for the well pump that they had already shut off. I hoped all the best for the owners and wondered where they had gone, and I hoped it wasn't to the FEMA shelter. Although if they had stayed here, they would likely have been killed by those two bad guys.

There was another neighbor about a mile further down the road, but I thought I had been gone long enough, and I walked back home. When Amy met me she had a sad look on her face. At least until I told her the other neighbors had left and had likely gone to be with family somewhere. "Good for them" was what she said and I could see the relief in her expression.

We both stayed home for the next couple weeks. I helped Amy with the garden some days until she would chase me out. I am not a good gardener. I did make a marker for the graves of Betty and Frank which I placed on their grave.

Summer came, and the garden required more and more work. Amy let me help her but only under her watchful eye. We were soon harvesting the early plants from the garden with more things getting ripe all the time. Though Amy had a good supply of seeds left she said this year she would harvest some of the seeds from the plants we now had growing. This meant that some had to be allowed to go-to-seed.

She told me that the seed she planted was called "heirloom" seeds which allowed seed harvesting without worry of what the next year's plants would produce. She said most of the regular seeds you buy in small packets in stores often don't produce the same plants again from harvested seed. I didn't understand, but I believed what she said. It was one of her areas of expertise.

We still listened to the TV news broadcasts mainly to get the weather reports and just to hear another voice. The broadcasted news was rather bizarre. It said nothing about the loss of electric power or phone systems or the internet. Instead, it reported how well FEMA was helping those few Americans in need with food and shelter. The news also talked about rebuilding projects and how farmers had put in huge crops this year from which the government predicted record harvests. Neither Amy nor I believed a single word we heard on the news. The weather reports, on the other hand, were the same as always with them getting it correct sometimes and wrong other times.

    I did make the hike to the third neighbor's place. I found it empty also and did shut off the main electric breaker before I left. While there I noticed that they had several mature fruit trees in their yard which I made a mental note of to come back in the late summer to harvest what fruit there was so it did not go to waste.

    I also checked the other two neighbors' places for fruit trees and found additional trees that had fruit growing on them. Also at two of the places, I found old gardens from last year that had a few volunteer plants growing in them. Some of which were ready, so I picked what I could from them to bring home.

    It was obvious that our own fruit trees would produce much more fruit this year simply because the trees were maturing. While working in our garden I often looked hungrily at our orchard waiting for everything to ripen. Amy was a wise woman and had carefully picked which fruit varieties to plant. She had early, mid-season, and late ripening varieties of most of the different fruits. This meant everything wasn't all ripe at once and instead you could pick fruits for a much longer time span.

    When the first of our fruit started ripening, I made a point to check the neighbors' fruit trees also. I picked fruit at those places also. Between all four places, we had quite a lot of fruit. It was a major effort to process all the fruit we had available thanks to harvesting it from four places. It made me wonder just how many other places were empty with all the fruit just going to waste. What a shame.

We canned, froze, ate, and dried fruit over a two-month time period. I really liked the fruit much better than the garden produce, but I did eat some of everything, except spinach! It must be an acquired taste I guess. Though I think Amy snuck it in some of the meals, she made and didn't tell me so I would eat what she made. She is a very pretty and clever woman. And I believe she has the capability to be devious.

Our wild meat supply was all gone now. When I got the opportunity one day, I shot a small buck deer that was looking for a way to get at our fruit trees. He was small enough so we could easily process the meat quickly and soon all the fresh venison was in our freezer. Except for the fresh chops, I made on the grill for supper that night. The young deer was both tasty and tender and way better than what canned meat we had left.

Both Amy and I decided we needed to kill more wild game this fall and winter than we had last year. When Amy had stocked up with food before the collapse, she had bought quite a lot of commercially canned meat of different kinds. We still had a fair amount but when that was gone that would be the end of it for a long time we expected. So that led to our decision to harvest more wild meat.

The jerky we made last season was good, and because of that, it did not last us very long. This year we planned to jerk a much bigger supply. That would also free up enough room in our large chest freezer for more frozen meat.

Thinking about food we both decided to "harvest" any food items that were still viable at all the neighbors' houses. We took the pickup and went through all three of the closest places on the same day. We found a fair amount of things like spices, flour, sugar, salt, and mixed other items. Much of what we found we deemed not to be edible any longer. Some of what we did not take might have still been fine to eat, but we just could not take any chances on either of us getting sick.

While at the houses we did also did a quick check for other items that could be valuable to us. Mainly this just meant looking in medicine cabinets for medical supplies. We did not want to steal, but we did not want items that were now very valuable (like food) to just go to waste. We didn't take anything like clothes or jewelry or anything like that. I admit we did borrow quite a few books but those we had every intention of returning after we read them. We had another long winter coming, and from last winter we learned that any book would be highly desired.

Chapter 18

Winter came just like we knew it would. Before any major snowfall, we had killed three full sized elk and a deer. Most of the meat was frozen, but this year we did make a relatively huge amount of jerky also. We tried several recipes when making the jerky, mostly just to give us some variety. We also harvested five turkeys and a few rabbits. I also shot a few squirrels so Amy could try them to see if she liked the taste. She was reluctant to eat them, but when she did, she found that the meat didn't taste bad at all. There was just not very much of it. Squirrel tastes a hundred times better than spinach.

Late in the fall, I had harvested some more firewood. We had a chainsaw along with plenty of gas and oil for it. I do admit that I don't care for putting up firewood. We still had plenty on hand, but neither of us knew just how long we could depend on the gas we had stored to stay viable to use in small engines like the chainsaw. So I brought home several loads of firewood using my truck and trailer to reduce the number of trips and to save fuel. I ended up bringing home more than we had used last winter, so it was a net gain from when all this started. I tried to stack the new firewood out of the way so it could "season," and we would use stored firewood this winter.

Cutting and splitting firewood can be dangerous work and I was very careful not to get hurt. There was no hospital around, no ambulance service, and no way to call for help anyway. But I made it through with no real mishaps, so we counted our blessings.

The winter is long. Thank goodness we 'borrowed' all the books from the neighbors. We hardly even looked at the titles of the books we brought home because we both knew by the end of winter we would each read anything and everything. Last winter we had even carefully read every ad in every magazine we had in the house. Besides books, we had also borrowed all the magazines we could find at our neighbors. Good thing too because in the middle of winter both the TV and the single radio station went off the air. There was no warning and no reason that we know of for the abrupt end of the broadcasts. We couldn't do anything about it and we then really dug into our fresh supply of books and magazines.

      Like all winters this one slowly, ever so slowly ended like winters have done for centuries. We were both more than ready for spring to arrive. One thing we both regretted was that we did not borrow the stationary exercise bike that was at one of the houses. It looked old but had obviously seen very little use like most exercise equipment people buy. Instead, we had just made up different exercises for us to do at home.

      Amy had a couple of exercise videos that we watched and exercised to on many days. We both got to the point that we knew every word and grunt from the videos before they were heard. After a while we stopped using the videos and just made up our own different programs. We made it fun and tried many different things. Staying in shape was now not just something desirable but could easily be life-saving also to us.

      When all the broadcasts had ended, we still would check a couple of times every day to see if they had started up again. At least at first we did. Then we checked once a day and then once every couple days. Then it was whenever we happened to think about checking. When spring arrived, it was even longer spans before we would check the TV or the radio.

      When Amy tried the TV one night, she actually jumped when there was a broadcast playing.

"This message will repeat continuously until replaced by new announcements.

"People of the United States. I am a military liaison officer whose job is to communicate and coordinate words and actions between the Armed Forces and our civilian government. My current assignment is to give all citizens an update on previous and current actions in this nation. Our country is still intact, but there have been some changes to our leadership. Though many of you did not hear about it, approximately one year ago the President and the Vice President of the United States were assassinated by unknown assailants. The people responsible were never caught and are still at large to our knowledge.

"At that point, the Presidency went to the next in line which was the Speaker of the House of Representatives. At that time the Speaker took the oath of office and then assumed the role of President of the United States. Even though the federal government at that time was constantly broadcasting over both TV and radio, no announcement was made to the American people about this terrible tragedy and the change in leadership. And even to date, this has never been announced, until now.

"It was also never announced over the airwaves that the new President with the backing of Congress immediately declared Martial Law over the whole nation for the first time in history. This declaration gave the federal government immense powers over the people. Also through several Presidential Proclamations and Executive Orders, this new President assumed, even more, power over the people of the United States.

"At that time many people throughout the nation were rounded up and placed in "emergency shelters." These, for the most part, turned out to be much more like the gulags of the Soviet Union. Citizens were welcomed in but were not allowed to leave. Obviously, this went against everything America has ever stood for in its whole history.

"I am here to say that these despicable actions forced on the American by their own government have now ended. The former Speaker of the House and who was your President has been displaced from his position as President through the actions of many brave men and women of our Armed Forces. Unfortunately, the President did not survive this action.

"As per the laws of this nation, the next in line for the Presidency would be the President pro tempore of the Senate. This person was located and accepted the immense burden of the Presidency. I am here to tell you that you now have a new President.

"Your new President's first action was to remove the declaration of Martial Law and all the Presidential Proclamations and Executive Orders of the former President. America is again the Land of the Free. All of the so-called "emergency shelters" have opened their barb wire covered doors and citizens can come and go as they please. These places no longer have to be feared by American citizens.

"However all is not roses in your once great nation. Countless citizens have died. And honestly, I fear more will die before we can turn things around again and set everything right. We all have much work ahead to rebuild this nation. Soon we will make additional announcements on how you might help with this process. As I speak, many actions are currently taking place to ease the suffering of many of our citizens. This is and will continue to be our main goal.

"Some of you will see the results of these actions soon if you haven't already. There is much more to come, and further announcements will be made in a timely manner.

"Thank you for your time and may God Bless You and may God Bless America."

"This message will repeat continuously until replaced by new announcements."

Both Amy and I listened to the same announcement again without speaking. We wanted to make sure we missed nothing. When the announcement was completed for the second time, Amy shut the TV off. Then we both just sat without talking trying to absorb everything we had just been told.

Chapter 19

"Well, that was interesting."

"Well, that is an understatement."

"There has to be so much work to do. It's hard to comprehend it all."

"Where to even start would be a hard decision to make."

"Well, it sure cannot all be fixed overnight. Even the guy said he expected more deaths."

"And we are assuming this is all on the up and up and it might not be."

"The guy seemed sincere."

I think a wait and see attitude is the best step for a while."

"But we could help with the rebuilding!"

"What we need to do is take care of ourselves first. Plant a big garden and do what we have to do to feed ourselves so we will not be a burden on others. Wait and see what develops while looking after ourselves. Then only after we have our own food secured and we learn more can we maybe help others."

"I guess that does make sense. We could hardly help others if we need help ourselves."

So that is what we did. When it warmed enough, we again planted a big garden. And yes Amy planted more spinach. By this time I had learned at least a little bit from Amy, and she did not chase me out of the garden anymore, or at least not often.

We listened to the news every night, but it was at least a month before the original broadcast was even changed. It was always just repeating every single day all day long. When the broadcast did change, it was just more or less a pep talk for the American people with no real update on what was happening.

It was maybe two weeks or more before there was another change in the broadcast. This time there was some real information. One thing they said was to tune into the radio where you could receive much more localized information for your own area. Which did make sense to us.

They also said power was being restored as fast as possible with many areas already up and running. We also learned that some areas of the nation had never lost power. Unfortunately, power lines were down due to storms in many rural areas, and that would be slow to get all that fixed. This too made sense and would be expected to happen.

We worked every day on our own place and did what we could to bolster our own supplies. With the garden in full swing and vital to our own survival we had no choice but to stay and make sure we had a good harvest.

And like last year as the garden slowly petered out we switched over to harvesting fruit. This year there was even more than last because of more of our many trees maturing. And again we harvested from the trees on all the surrounding empty places. When I remembered a dehydrator that I saw in one of the houses I brought it to our place and used it to increase our drying capacity which was sorely needed.

We did listen to the TV news station and had also been listening to a local radio station as soon as one was up and running. The TV news now started to have video footage of some cities and showed many things both bad and good.

Very large mass gravesites were shown. Obviously, this was done on purpose. It showed that many had died but also that many survived. Satellite photos were shown of nighttime pictures of the United States both before the events and currently. The difference was vividly different. The lights were everywhere in the before pictures and scattered in the current pictures. But it did show that most parts of the country now had power again.

We finally saw our President. He made announcements about once every week. He seemed like a sad and no-nonsense guy. He also said that as soon as possible we would have elections and he would not be on the ballot. He would work now and do his level best for all of America, but he was ready to turn the job over to someone else. Someone the American people elected for that job.

Again as soon as it was cool enough, I shot a deer which we processed immediately. Later with a little cooler weather, we shot elk to fill our freezer and assure our food supply. Then we were ready to help with our own food supply stored and ready. When the radio announced a general meeting in the city closest to us, we decided to make the trip. We both decided to offer up our help if we were needed.

The meeting was to commence not at night like in the old days but at noon instead. The noon start would allow folks to come in the daylight and leave in the daylight and be held during the warmest part of the day. Someone with some common sense was likely now in charge I thought.

We took Amy's SUV this time. Though both vehicles had been started on a regular basis so we could have used either. We brought extra work clothes and a fair supply of food along with other supplies. If needed we could start working immediately and stay for awhile using our own supplies.

The meeting was well attended. Some drove cars and trucks to attend with others walking to the meeting hall, and others were riding horses to attend. Almost everyone was armed with at least a handgun. There was no trouble of any kind, and everyone seemed polite and almost relieved to be there.

In charge was the 'acting' mayor. He made it plain he was not elected and just kind of 'took over' the job that no one wanted. He asked that if time permitted and if agreeable to those present a new mayor could be elected today to replace him.

Also present were a few Army personnel. The meeting was mostly just an update of what had been done so far and what was needed to be done as soon as possible, and then things that many hoped would be done soon. Questions were taken and sometimes those in the audience were asked to share any ideas they might have to get things moving in the right direction.

There was no yelling (other than a few cheers), and it was one of the smoothest meetings Amy and I had ever attended. There were no demands. No one yelled at anyone for any reason. People waited to talk until they were called upon. Most had something worthwhile to say when they did speak.

By the time the meeting ended the acting mayor was turned into the elected mayor, something that he seemed to expect but which did not seem to make him happy when it happened. With the breakup of the meeting, people in charge of certain work groups were pointed out and separated so they could have their own short meetings with those that needed help or wished to supply help.

Amy and I offered our assistance, and our help was quickly accepted. There would be no payment of any kind though we could stay in the gym at the high school which had many cots set up for that purpose. The power was on in most of the city, and they had running clean water, and the sewer system was again functional for most of the city including the school.

We checked out the high school and found that it was set up fairly well having been used many times in past years as an emergency shelter used during wildfires and other disasters. That is where we stayed for the next five days while we worked. We did receive a coupon for fuel and filled the gas tank before we left town. We both wanted to get back and check on our place but promised to return the following week.

And that is how it worked until we had major snowfall. We ended up working a total of twenty-one days. At that time we just stayed home for the remainder of the winter. We at least had done some work before being trapped at home for the winter. While some roads would be plowed during winter those in outlying areas like ours would not be plowed. There were no complaints. It was what it was, and people including us understood that simple fact.

Chapter 20

Work was being done all throughout the winter months across the nation. Maybe not so much in the northern rural areas but in cities and in the southern locations where winters were not so bad. And Congress was busy the whole time. There was no time off for them, and they remained in session every week where they met at least five days out of every seven.

The President worked closely with the Congress, and there were no vetoes, and many bills were passed. All were passed on bi-partisan votes and quickly signed by the President. One such bill created a new currency and did away with the old currency.

The new currency would not be a fiat one like the old dollar. It would be backed by gold and silver like the nation's money had originally been designed and what had always been the law. That law had just been ignored for over a hundred years. There would be no Federal Reserve Bank anymore. That was now dissolved.

The new currency looked somewhat like the old dollars. The backs of each of the bills were gold instead of green to signify the backing of gold. The price of gold was at least temporarily set at thirteen hundred of the new dollars. And the exchange rate for old dollars to new was set at twenty-five to one. You would get four new dollars for every one hundred old dollars turned in.

Old coins would have the same exchange rates. The old money had to be exchanged within four months, after which it would only have sentimental value. New coins would be minted. The new coins would contain silver or gold similar to coins minted in our nation's past. The new coins would not be pure silver or gold for durability reasons.

    The new pennies and nickels would be minted from a strong copper alloy. There was some talk of a possible half-cent coin, but Congress decided to wait and see if that was needed before going to the expense of minting any. Coins minted would be pennies, nickels, dimes, quarters, dollars, and ten dollars. Printed money would consist of one, five, ten, twenty, and fifty dollar bills. Coins and bills might be dropped or others added as per demand in the future.

    The stock markets would remain closed for an indefinite period. There was talk of not even allowing corporations again. Banks would be checked by the government and for the time being would only be able to loan money on a one for one basis. In other words, they would have to have all the money on hand to lend out; they would not be able to leverage their money or assets. Possibly that would change in the future.

    The federal government would shrink down to a fraction of its former size. All government entities would shrink or disappear. Taxes would resume after the first of the next year. There was much work to be done to figure out taxes at all levels of government. Taxes were necessary but would have to be handled much better than in the past.

    Congress finally voted in term limits. Two terms maximum the same as the President. Congress also wanted to place term limits on all elected positions at all levels of government down to county dog catcher but decided to leave that to the states and local governments to do for themselves. Congress did place term limits on all judges including the Supreme Court which had a ten-year limit.

    The number of changes being made was staggering and seemingly never-ending. Huge sections of the Federal government were disbanded and most responsibility given to the states or just dropped entirely. Congress had finally learned to cut and not just spend. They even cut their own wages and benefits for the first time ever.

Amy and I tried to keep up with everything that was happening, but it was almost totally mind-boggling. There were just so many changes happening so fast. Granted these changes needed to be done and should have been done many years ago.

And we were starting to have hope. Hope for the future. For our nation and us. Gradually businesses opened or in a few cases re-opened. Most were completely new businesses though. People at first were very leery of the new money. At first, many would only exchange old money for the new coins that contained real precious metal. Gradually the paper money did take off just because it was handier to carry.

With the huge difference in exchange rate, there was not all that much money to carry around anyway. Many items were priced at the half-cent because of the exchange rate. So far people were just working out the pricing and the buying of goods and services. There were plenty of bumps on this road, but it gradually smoothed out over time.

After winter both Amy and I took regular jobs. We talked about moving closer to town. There were plenty of empty houses and thanks to Amy converting most of our money into precious metals we now had money available to us. But even we had bumps in the road.

One of these bumps was Amy's tummy. It was already showing, and I was trying to get her to stop working. But I finally gave that up. She is…let's just say a very determined and strong-willed woman. But she is my woman, and soon she will be a mother, and I'll be a father.

Life is good.

The End

Mountain Hideaway
by

Pete Thorsen

Thank you for reading this short story of mine, and I hope you found it enjoyable. If it was something you liked, please watch for more of my stories to follow. Below are some of my already published stories that you might also enjoy. So far I have well over 50 stories published on Kindle with most also available in print. My success is totally the result of you, my readers, and you have my most deep felt Thank You!

Pete Thorsen

America on Fire

Four complete stories of apocalyptic disasters that befall the citizens of the United States by one of America's popular apocalyptic fiction writers. Read how some Americans rise to meet the challenges and fight to survive when disaster strikes the whole country.

In **Finding Hope,** a deadly pandemic sweeps the globe resulting in the deaths of a large amount of the world population. One man finds a purpose to his life when he finds and befriends a little girl.

In **Three Strikes And You're Out America,** three nuclear EMP missiles explode high above the United States it causes extreme devastation by taking out the whole electric grid and all electronics.

In **An Economic Firestorm,** the economic collapse of the US Dollar and the economy of the USA are lived through by a family in rural Arizona.

In **Thar She Blows,** see what happens to a few groups of people when the Yellowstone Caldera erupts and devastates a huge portion of the United States.

Disaster in America

Four complete stories of apocalyptic disasters that befall the citizens of the United States by one of America's most popular apocalyptic fiction writers. Read how some Americans rise to meet the challenges and fight to survive when disaster strikes.

In **What? The sun did all this,** a massively strong CME that strikes the earth destroying the electric grid and most electric devices. One man attempts to reunite with his scattered family.

In **Surviving in Trying Times,** one middle-aged couple try to cope with what becomes something like the second great depression.

In **Relax It's Just the Flu,** a massive pandemic of a deadly strain of the flu wreaks havoc to the USA. This story follows a few of the survivors.

In **Global Warming (It's real this time),** a young man struggles to survive twenty years after a man-made accident does cause massive global warming.

Survival in America

Four complete early stories from one of America's most popular apocalyptic writers.

No Electric Survival, is a story of the aftermath of a severe EMP that shuts down the nation's electric power grid and makes most vehicles unusable.

Rural Dollar Collapse, when there is a complete collapse of the US economy this story shows how members of one family cope with what happens in their areas of the once great United States.

Pandemic to a New Beginning, is a story that follows the lives of two young people before and after a deadly flu pandemic sweeps around the globe causing a severe drop in the world population.

No Economic Collapse in the Woods, centers on three people that are strangers to each other but find strength when circumstances throw them together, and they try to live their lives in the bleak new world after the US Dollar collapses.

Trouble in America

Five complete early stories from one of America's most popular apocalyptic writers.

How I Survived WW3, is a story that follows a regular working man that happens to survive World War Three after making just a few preparations.

The Carrington Event Revisited, is the story of a catastrophic solar coronal mass ejection event similar to the one that hit the Earth in 1859.

A Collapse to a Fresh Start, is a story of two young people who make their way out of Chicago and run to a very rural area of Colorado when they feel the United States is about to suffer an economic collapse and possibly change forever.

A Midwest Homestead, follows the lives of a young couple in Minnesota who through determination and hard work build their little homestead that is their salvation in a time chaos.

An Oklahoma Retreat, is the story of a widely scattered family that all return to the original family ranch in Oklahoma when the United States falls on very bad times.

The End of America

Five complete early stories from one of America's most popular apocalyptic writers.

An Arizona Haven, is a story of how a will to overcome obstacles and some common sense can mean all the difference in your very survival in this case after an EMP has shut down the whole power grid.

Dystopia USA, is the tale of a possible very dark future in the great United States of America.

The Zombie Plague, is a story of a plague that is affecting the whole world and changing people drastically into something that is not quite human.

Living Through the Collapse, is about the economic collapse of the economy of the USA as lived through by a family in rural Minnesota.

Polar Shift, is about two good friends and their lives before and after a major catastrophic event that changes the whole world and causes chaos.

Catastrophe In America

Four complete stories from one of America's most popular apocalyptic writers.

Hard Times. After multiple terrorist attacks and a collapsing economy, the incoming hurricane is the last straw, and a man flees his town for someplace safe to ride out the coming chaos.

From Civilized to Barbaric! When the electric power goes out and does not appear to be coming back on a man tries to flee New York City to try and find a safe haven.

Cruel End to a Great Country. Follow the life of a simple janitor after the nation's economy gradually winds down to a complete stop.

Just Another Day. While family from another state are visiting an EMP changes everything. See how this now extended family copes with what has happened.

America in Ruins

Four complete stories from one of America's most popular apocalyptic writers.

The Cruel New World. When a magnetic storm destroys most all electrical equipment in the world, it proves to be a severe catastrophic event. This story follows a gun as it changes owners in the violent new world.

Relax, It's Just the Flu! When a deadly a strain of the flu devastates the population, a small band of survivors struggles to survive.

Nice Day for Armageddon. When a foreign country hits the United States with multiple EMP's the population of this once great nation fights to survive.

A Brutal Reset. When our nation's economy crashes those people wishing for a reset of our society get their wish. Now we have brutal violence and starvation where it is a struggle every day just to survive.

Devastated America

Four complete stories from one of America's most popular apocalyptic writers.

The End Times. Two people from vastly different walks of life do what they can to survive after America tears itself apart from within.

The Good Sam. A young couple living in a small rural community thinks that they might be immune from the rash of brutal violence that as swept across the whole nation after terrorists take down the power grid but discover the hard way that is just not the case.

Bound for Home.   A man finds himself almost two thousand miles from home when a terrorist attack cripples the nation's whole system infrastructure and he makes a perilous journey back to his home.

One Man's Path. When the sun cripples all mankind a man loses his family and searches for a new path and reason to go on.

Calamity in America

Three complete stories from one of America's most popular apocalyptic writers.

Stormy Weather. The story of a young man living in Nebraska on his now small family farm who fights for survival after America falls apart.

After the 2nd Great Depression. Eight years after the fall of our nation America is quite a different place. It's a place where every person must be hard and strong just to try and continue living.

A Girl's Gotta Survive. A young girl learns to fight to live in the circumstances she finds life has dealt her. Will her life ever get any better?

Doomsday for America

Three complete stories from one of America's most popular apocalyptic writers.

Dark Days. When hackers take out the nation's power grid, a young man and his family in Colorado try to cope with the loss of power.

A Bright New Beginning. An ex-military man now seeks nothing but peace. Then the US economy crashes and his peace is put on hold.

A Sunny Disaster. A man retires on a remote property and finds he likes living now as a hermit. Will his lonesome life change when a solar CME shuts off the nation's power grid?

Re-set for America

Three complete stories from one of America's most popular apocalyptic writers.

Viral Survival   When a viral outbreak decimates the population of all the countries of the world a young couple in a northern state in the America tries to weather the resulting hardships.

A Rocky Demise   A bitter man and a lonely woman barely start their lives together when twin asteroids strike the Earth causing an incredible disaster.

A Hard Fall   This is one family's story of living through a drastic catastrophe that affects the whole United States forcing the population to live without electric power.

Upheaval in America

Three complete stories from one of America's most popular apocalyptic writers.

When The Bottom Fell Out   A husband and wife take their young son and move from the big city life to a very rural house in Idaho. This forces big changes in their lifestyle. When the economy goes south, the couple is happy they did make those changes.

A Nation In Trouble   A drifter who could care less about the economy is like most people in America, but they all find out just how bad things can get when the economy collapses.

Lonely Road South   A man is forced to learn a lot, even about himself, when a solar flare takes out the power grid in America.

The Lottery Winner

When Jake wins the lottery, it changes his life. And his life needs changing too as a somewhat screwed up veteran. He starts to get his head on straight and then the nation's economy starts to crumble. As things get worse and worse, Jake tries to think of ways to stay ahead of the game. He has fought battles before; this one is just different. It is not his style to give up, and he is determined to go down fighting every inch of the way.

Cincinnati Shutdown

This is a story of a teenager becoming a man over several years during increasingly bad economic times in the city of Cincinnati. With the living conditions in the city gradually growing worse as deteriorating conditions start slowly and gradually gets worse as the young man grows up. He does what he can to protect his family and the girl he loves.

Korean Chaos

Lars and his family feel safe in their rural house in the middle of America. But with North Korea constantly threatening the United States and now knowing that Korea does have long range ICBM's and the nukes to fit them, things seem much more serious. So together the married couple decides to take a few precautions for 'just in case.' The question is have they done enough and done it soon enough? Can they protect their young daughter if something does happen?

Trouble
In Texas

A drifter who stops near a Texas city finds a good job and decides to stay, at least for awhile. And that's where he finds himself when a deadly pandemic sweeps across the globe. Texas is not spared and this one man does what he can to survive the deadly disease. The disease kills hundreds of millions of people around the world, will this one man survive? Will he even want to survive when so many others are dead?

Made in the USA
San Bernardino, CA
14 February 2018